y'all chose this

The Diaries of Trina Pardo

a novel

y'all chose this

The Diaries of Trina Pardo

a novel

Dorcas Renee

Y'all Chose This! The Diaries of Trina Pardo

Copyright ©2024 by Dorcas Renee

ISBN: 979-8-218-50787-9

Printed in the United States of America.

Find out more at dorcacsrenee.com

Prologue

Aunt Poohpie had built up a tolerance to the narcotic over the past months, so it took a few minutes for the drug to take effect. Once it did, the family exploded into action, preparing to flee. Beans kissed Poohpie on the forehead then turned to leave too when she stubbed her toe on something hard. She fell on top of the unconscious woman and saw the corner of a box peeking from under the bed. When she saw the writing scrawled a top the box, Beans was flooded with a memory from her childhood:

***

Beans had come running into the living room when she heard Poohpie screaming. Relieved to find that this was the sound of joy—not pain, she asked what was so funny. Poohpie just screamed "I'm gonna pee my pants!" and ran to the bathroom dropping a Tweety Bird yellow, leather-bound journal on the floor at Beans' feet.

Not thinking, Beans picked up the book and began reading.

"Dear Diary, last night Sandra called and long and the short of it… we are going to be RICH!"

RICH??! Beans knew she shouldn't read further but curiosity got the best of her:

"Last night San asked, 'Do you ever want to just chew but you are not hungry?'"

"Yeah, all the time. You just want the sensation and the taste of food" I said.

"Wouldn't it be great if there was something you could chew but you didn't have to eat it? It wouldn't be *food* . . . just something to *chew*." she said.

"Like a chew toy but not!"

"RIIIIIGHT! It could have different flavors and everything."

"RightRightRightRight . . . So you could chew and taste something but not swallow it.

"YeahYeahYeah! Cuz sometimes you just want to chew . . . "

" . . . But you're don't wanna EAT."

"YES!"

"Oh! Oh! You know what we could call it? Mastikibble. Cuz you masticate it," I said.

" . . . But you don't eat it—like kibble!" San said.

"That's genius!" we both said.

We talked for three hours about Mastikibble. What flavors. How to market it. Everything. I barely slept! We still have to figure out how to make it but . . . We are going to be SO RICH! Like millionaires.

I keep thinking of different flavors. We could have sweet potato pie, Apple pie. I don't know about a beef flavored one. That might taste nasty after a minute. But you know what? We COULD have like a MINTY flavored one. Like . . . like . . . Doublemint! Yeah! Is double a kind of mint?

Wait. Doublemint.

Mastikibble is Chewing gum.

Shit!

Beans doubled over laughing. When she straightened up, Poohpie was standing right in front of her, face tight. Instantly the laughter died in Beans' throat.

"I'm sorry Poohpie! I shouldn't have read your diary! I'm sorry!"

Poohpie sat down next to Beans, took the journal from her hands and put it in her purse.

"Diaries are private Beans. Full of things I don't always want to share. Now you know something about me that was just for me to know," she said.

Poohpie was right. Beans felt privileged to know that much about her aunt and afraid that she had crossed the line. Would Poohpie ever trust her? Beans had never seen Poohpie mad or disappointed in her. She didn't know what to do or expect so she just sat there.

After a while, Beans looked up into Poohpie's face and said, "Mastikibble!"

Poohpie and Beans burst into hysterical laughter again.

***

"Beans! Hurry up! We have to leave before the patrollers get here!" Beans' mom yelled from upstairs, reminding Beans that the family was being hunted, and that Poohpie was being left behind. She dumped the contents of the box into a tote bag and ran up the stairs leaving the empty box marked,

"THESE ARE THE DIARIES OF TRINA PARDO."

Part I

. . . . too bad the heart is freaking stupid.

1

Dear Diary,

Thank you, Dr. Ira Progoff, for popularizing journal writing. Because of you I have a place to record my thoughts and feelings. Because of you I can admit that in my heart I am *Such* a whiney little bitch, without fear that anyone will know.

Whiney because:

My family is not making a big enough deal about the fact that I was just offered—and accepted- my DREAM JOB! It just garnered what felt like an obligatory "That's great Trina" full stop. No exclamation point. No "tell me more!" Just a "Maybe you'll finally be able to move into your own apartment!" Yes, exclamation point. The "and stop being a loser"—although implied was not stated.

Bitch because:

I left the room and cried bitter tears because, after that last statement, the conversation turned to an animated discussion, full of exclamation points, about what we were going to do for my niece's graduation . . . from kindergarten.

Whiney little bitch!

Me. Not my niece.

I wonder if Progoff championed journaling because he had too many whiney, bitchy clients like me.

THE ASSIGNMENT TWO:

KEEP YOUR ENEMIES CLOSER

Darrius Jerome Gourdine,
DJG Enterprises

Cover Design: Paul Woodruff

Book layout and design: Norman Rich

Author photography by James McDuff Photography

For book signings and speaking engagements, send all inquiries to darrius@iamassigned.com.

All scriptural references are taken from the New King James version of the Holy Bible.

www.iamassigned.com

ISBN: 978-0-9755660-7-7

"And from the days of John the Baptist until now, the Kingdom of Heaven suffereth violence, and the violent take it by force." — Matthew 11:12 (KJV)

"I wish each of you much success! I wish you as many years as these Agency success stories that you just heard from! I wish to thank each of your Chief Presenters, I salute you!" He waves toward the upper tiers of the arena. "To your trainers, I salute you all! Thank you for the hard work that you do to make all our lives a little more comfortable! Now, let's get out there and work our assignments!"

With that, Dr. Weincaster steps back from the podium to a standing ovation. Amidst all the clapping and cheering, I know that every new inductee is as anxious as I am to receive our assignments. Whatever my assignment is, I hope I have it for ten million years. I want to be on stage behind a keynote speaker and awe the audience with how long I've been on earth after my death.

Another man steps to the microphone as the applause begins to dwindle for Dr. Weincaster. He is a much shorter man and has to bend the microphone down in order to speak into it. "Thank you Dr. Weincaster for those stirring words. You always encourage us toward the bettering of our future and we thank you." Everyone takes their seats. "To the new inductees, you have successfully completed your courses here at The Agency and we congratulate you. Now is the time you've all been waiting for. We know each of you is anxious to find out what your assignment is and we don't wish to delay you any further. Your Chief Presenter was given an envelope while Dr. Weincaster was speaking. Inside that envelope is your assignment. Your Chief Presenter gave you instructions as to where to meet him or her after this ceremony. It is now after the ceremony. Feel free to get your assignment! Congratulations!"

Before the word congratulations leaves his lips, a new inductee seated toward the front leaps up and starts to make his way toward his Chief Presenter. With that, everyone gets up and begins quickly moving. It's like mayhem as we're all desperately trying to get to our CP. For the first time since being introduced to The Agency, it seems as if there is total chaos. Everything with The Agency is well organized and structured. Now the new inductees are running and almost falling over one another to get their assignment. I am as well.

Alexander, Kevin and Josh are smiling as I approach. Kevin is actually laughing at me. I find no humor yet his laughter causes me to laugh as well. "So, you ready to get your assignment?" Alexander is waving my envelope from side to side as he speaks to me with a smile.

"Stop playing with me!" I say smiling but with all seriousness.

"Here you go. Be careful opening it, I don't want you to tear the letter in half!" Alexander hands me the envelope. I turn it over. The envelope is sealed with The Agency logo and is signed across the seal by Dr. Weincaster. I assume that is to ensure that the envelope hasn't been opened by none other than the intended new inductee. I carefully break the seal and take out the folded paper. I drop the envelope onto the floor.

"Read it out loud." Alexander says.

"From The Council of..." I skip that part. "Dear Mr. Brian Lampkin. It is indeed our pleasure to welcome you as a new member of The Agency. We are proud that you have decided to prolong your stay on Earth and work along with our dedicated team. It is our intent that you have a long career with us and we hope that is your intent as well. Once again, on behalf of the entire Council and all the members of The Agency, welcome."

I read the next paragraph. "Your assignment. You are to meet Angela Renee Hamilton. She is a single, twenty-seven year old African American female. She has been praying earnestly for a husband. We have purposely designed you to be the husband she has been asking for. Your assignment is to meet Ms. Hamilton and cause her to fall in love with you. You will ask Ms. Hamilton to marry you, making her Angela Renee Lampkin. You are then to ensure that Mrs. Angela Renee Lampkin, all of your children and all of your grandchildren go to Hell."

I look up from the letter and stare at Alexander. He seems speechless. I look back at the letter to make sure I read correctly what I just read out loud. I look up again and back at Alexander. "Wait... what?"

"What? Let me see that!" Alexander says. Before I can respond, he snatches the letter out of my hand. As Alexander looks it over, I stare at him in a state of disbelief and shock. I watch him read it as if I can see every word that I just read register in his mind.

Both Kevin and Josh are watching me for my next move. I see now why they put security measures in place. If I decide to flip out, they will take me down immediately.

Alexander looks up from the letter and smiles. "Well, well, well... I had no idea I was in the presence of greatness!" He says.

"Wh... what?" I say.

"You're the primary on an interactive assignment! Wow, I didn't realize you had it in you Brian but I'm definitely impressed."

"I don't know what you're talking about but you need

to stop talking in riddles and codes and tell me what's up!" I've been anxious and nervous for months, trying to find out what my assignment is. Now that I've graduated from all of the classes, attended this ceremony today, and received my assignment on a polished letterhead, I hear something crazy. I'm trying to process this and hoping it is some sort of error.

"Okay, okay. There's a lot to explain. Come on, let's go." Alexander says.

"Where are we going?"

"We need to get out of here so we can sit down. I need to help you begin to process this."

With that, Alexander motions for the three of us to follow him. He starts to walk toward the door that we came in to enter the huge auditorium. I hear my name called behind me. I'm in such a daze, I don't turn to acknowledge it until my name is called a second time. Not sure if I hesitated because of what I just learned about my assignment or the fact that my name has never been Brian and now everyone refers to me as such. I turn and see Suzanne, the new inductee who was in training with me. She and her Chief Presenter and security are smiling and walking toward us.

"Hey! I'm going to be a Chief Presenter!" Suzanne says excitedly.

I don't know what to say so I don't say anything. I look at her as if she just spoke to me in a language that I don't understand. I turn back to walk away when Alexander speaks for me.

"He's a primary on an important assignment. We need to go process it."

"Oh... say no more!" Suzanne's CP says in reply. Alexander spoke directly to Suzanne's Chief Presenter and not to Suzanne. What Alexander just said is completely understood by Suzanne's CP and she and Suzanne walk away. They are still smiling at one another. Suzanne is happy to become a Chief Presenter. Maybe she forgot that she's going to Hell at some point.

As we walk through the door, I see no one. There are hundreds of people around me. There are conversations that fill the entire capacity of the air around me. Yet, I neither see nor hear anyone. I feel like I'm in a fog and simply walking to keep from falling over. This entire process from the day that I died to this exact moment has been nothing short of crazy. Sentenced to a fate worst than death, tortured to have to endure while you wait for it, all while keeping your cool. Now that I have my assignment, I want to die all over again... but I don't want to go to Hell for not performing it. We are wading through a crowd of hundreds... maybe thousands of talking people. Alexander is in front of me, Josh and Kevin are behind me. Most people are standing around, while some are attempting to leave the building like we are.

This entire scene feels like a college graduation. A graduate gets his or her degree and proudly receives accolades from family and friends. New inductees are seemingly excited about receiving their assignments after weeks or training and waiting. Add a few horrendous and terrifying dreams and all seems well to new inductees. Except me. The only thing that seems more horrendous than my assignment is the thought of me refusing my assignment.

We finally make it out the front door of the building and find it a lot easier to walk. The four of us are silent as we walk to the SUV that has come to be my only form of transportation since my death. Josh takes the driver seat. Alexander sits in the back with me. He pulls out his cell phone and seems to read a text. He then looks up and speaks to Josh.

"Hit the Starbucks." Alexander says. Josh takes a left out of the parking lot in the direction of the Starbucks on Willingboro Parkway. As soon as he drives onto the main road, Alexander begins to speak to me. "What we found out in your assignment is that you're the primary person on an interactive project. In other words, there's a team of people you're going to be working with and you're the lead person."

"The lead person? What? What in the world does that mean and what kind of crazy assignment is this?" My voice is raised as I've been in a daze since I read my assignment. I'm just starting to come out of it and think about what it is that I read. I can feel myself start to tremble under the sound of my own voice. The enormous weight of what I read is now starting to settle on my shoulders.

"I've taken you as far as I'm supposed to. My assignment is pretty much over with you man. I'm gonna introduce you to the next person who'll take it over for you from here." Alexander says as he puts his hand on my leg to reassure me. "You'll be fine man. Remember, assignments are given out based on a person's purpose in their beforelife. You're built for this. I'm real proud of you."

"So wait? That's it? I won't see you guys ever again?" I ask.

"We'll definitely see each other, as long as you stay on this side of the table. Don't go back to Hell!"

Kevin laughs a little at Alexander's statement while still looking out the passenger side window.

"The next person who is going to help you is a part of the

12

team you're gonna lead. He just said he's at the Starbucks waiting on us. He'll take it from there and answer all your questions. You have a lot to get ready for so clear your mind of any of the shock from what you just learned and get ready. You got an important role my friend. I'll definitely see you around. Hey, you never know, I may bump into you from time to time." Alexander says with a smile.

"So where do you go next?"

"My next new inductee died yesterday. Josh, Kevin and I are going to meet him tonight. I'm waiting for my email confirmation of his address."

Alexander's statement causes me to feel dizzy. I feel like I may faint. This organization is so detailed that they already have the next person lined up for him.

"So who is the person I'm about to meet? Is he a Chief Presenter of some sort?"

"I don't know him. He's not a Chief Presenter, he's on your team. But he'll explain all that."

"And I won't need security anymore?"

"Nope. You're good. You're at the point now where The Agency can trust you. Once a new inductee completes the training process, they no longer need security unless there is some sort of problem or breach. You're good."

With that, the rest of the ride to Starbucks is silent. Not that I don't have more questions. I have over one million questions, but I can ask the next person that I'll be meeting in a few minutes. No point in continuing with Alexander. He's gotten me as far as he is assigned to. Now he's on to the next guy. I turn to look out my window. Watching my city... my home... where I worked... where I ate... where I partied.

Everything is so different now and I have to embrace it, or I'll never see it again and be wishing I still could.

Josh pulls into the parking lot of Starbucks. There's a parking spot right in the front. He takes it and puts the car in park.

"Alright man, on to your next phase. I'll walk you in."

All four of us open our doors. Once out of the SUV, Josh turns to me as I was sitting right behind him. "It's been good working with you man. Good luck with your assignment." He extends his hand to me. I take his hand firmly and shake it, looking him directly in the eyes. One of the character traits I learned early in my career is to shake hands firm with another man and look him in the eye. You can tell a lot about a man's strength by the way he shakes your hand.

"Thanks man. I appreciate all you shared with me these weeks." I reply.

"We know how it is. It's a lot to digest. Luckily for you, we didn't have to rough you up too bad." Josh laughs and I have to let out a laugh too. He's right and it is a funny statement.

I walk to the other side of the truck. Alexander is standing by the door of the Starbucks and allows me a moment to say goodbye to Kevin. When Kevin and I grab hands, he pulls me in to a half man hug. I pat him on the back.

"Hey man, it's been a pleasure. Do your thing and hopefully I'll see you around."

"Maybe in a thousand years." I say with a smile.

"Let's hope a thousand and another thousand!" He says back with a bigger smile.

Even though I smile, my mind and heart are in different

places. I haven't let go of the thought of my assignment. I'm supposed to meet a lady and cause her to fall in love with me. What man has ever been able to do that throughout the history of time? Then, I must guarantee that she, and all our kids and grandkids go to Hell. That is horrendous. If I don't, I go to Hell right now and I can't change my mind and come back.

Alexander opens the door for me and we walk into the Starbucks. There are a few people in line ready to place their order. There is a couple seated. There's a lady seated by herself using a laptop. There's another gentleman by himself reading a book. I don't know who I'm looking for so as always, I follow Alexander's lead.

"You want something?" he asks.

My first thought is hell no. I've learned however to go with the flow of this thing and I better get something. I might as well. "Pike Place Blend." I say.

"What?" Alexander asks.

"That's the name of what I want. It's called a Pike Place Blend."

"Oh okay. I forgot, you're a Starbucks coffee-a-nado or whatever." Alexander says. "Go grab that empty table over there and I'll be right back."

Alexander nods with his head to an empty table toward the left.

I thought we would walk up and meet the person we're here for right away. This operation seems so covert. I just follow along. As soon as I sit down, I look at each person in the Starbucks. The lady on her laptop is seated right across from me across the room. The man reading the book is in a more comfortable looking lounge chair toward the back. The couple are eating and not talking as he is typing on his phone and she looks frustrated that he is typing on his phone. I watch Alexander pay for our drinks. I remember the night I met him. He sat calmly in my room and knew I would freak out as he explained my fate. He is about to experience that all over again with a new person in a few hours. Alexander has become my best friend by default. He's walked me through this endless maze of emotions and questions. Now, I sit here looking to meet the next puzzle piece in my picture of my Afterlife.

"Alright." Alexander says as he sits down. "Your Pike drink is coming."

"Thanks. So you ready for your next new inductee?" I ask.

"Yeah. After a few times, it's almost routine. I'm still waiting on my email confirmation so we know where to go. Other than that, we'll be ready. Have to tell him what happened to him. Have to present him at training tomorrow. Have to sit through orientation. Blah blah blah."

"Wow." The routine has now become mundane to Alexander. Maybe it has to become mundane. This is how he keeps himself distracted from the reality of our future. I guess you have to do what you have to do to cope. I'm going to have to learn that.

"Hey man, I can't reiterate enough that you're gonna be fine. I have full confidence that you're gonna do well in your assignment. Just be yourself. Your assignment is already based on your purpose and who you already are. So don't worry about..." As Alexander is speaking, the manager of the Starbucks walks toward us holding two cups.

"OK guys, I have a Pike Blend for Brian and a Caramel for

Alexander." He says.

Alexander stands up and takes his cup. "OK Brian," he extends a hand toward me as I'm still seated. "Take care and call me if you need me."

"Wait... I thought I was supposed to meet someone here." I confusedly ask.

"You are. Here he is. His name is Randy."

Randy sits in the seat that Alexander just stood from. Alexander still has his hand extended. I'm trying to figure out how the Starbucks guy is the person I'm supposed to meet. Nonetheless, I take Alexander's hand and stand up. I pull him in for a hug and we embrace as if he was boarding a flight to Afghanistan for combat. "Thank you... for everything." I say.

"You're welcome bro. Stay strong. Complete your assignment." We back away from each other and I watch my Chief Presenter walk out of Starbucks.

Randy is a middle age Caucasian man. He is the manager of this Starbucks location. Although he's never taken my drink order, I know for sure I've said good morning. He smiles at me as he takes the seat that Alexander just occupied. "Brian, I'm Randy. Good to finally meet you."

"Finally? You work for..."

"The Agency? Yeah. I been with The Agency for a little over 3 years. I been waiting on you."

"Waiting on me? What are you talking about?" I ask. Randy slides my cup toward me on the table. I had totally forgotten that I ordered something to drink. I don't think I want it any longer.

"You're the primary in our operation. I can't do anything until you show up and get briefed on your part of the assignment. Once you're ready, the plan goes into effect." he says.

"I don't follow... at all." I say.

"My assignment is to help you with your assignment. I couldn't do that until you went through all the training and found out your role in the assignment. So I've literally been waiting all this time for whoever the primary person is so I can begin working my assignment."

There is a moment of silence. I'm trying to understand what Randy is explaining to me and allow it to sink in. He's been waiting over three years for me to show up and most of those three years, I hadn't even died yet.

Randy notices my silence and sees that I'm clearly confused. "There's a lot to digest and a lot of the obvious questions you have will be answered shortly. For now, we have an appointment. Let me go clock out and we can leave." Randy stands. "Don't let your Pike get cold."

"You can just leave work? Just like that?" I ask as he's walking toward the counter while untying his Starbucks apron.

"I already scheduled to have today off when I knew you would be finishing up. That's why I set your appointment for today. I only came in to meet you. I'll be right back."

Randy disappears behind the counter and through an employee only door. I'm still not sure what's happening. I look out the window to the parking lot. The SUV is gone. Alexander, Josh and Kevin are on to the next unlucky person. I suppose Suzanne is too. As Chief Presenter, she'll be doing what Alexander does. I hope she's good at it and doesn't get sent to Hell because her new inductee breaks under the pressure. I guess she's cut out for it since these assignments are based on your beforelife purpose.

By the time Randy returns, I've sipped my coffee. I might as well. He has his cell phone in his hand and he is texting as he walks up. I immediately remember that it was texting while driving that caused me to die in the first place. "Ready?" he asks as he steps to my table.

"I'm sure I don't have a choice."

Randy laughs. "No, you don't now that you mention it."

I pick up my cup and follow Randy outside the Starbucks. He takes out his key and turns off the alarm on his car. Randy drives a tan Honda Accord. We both get in and he starts the car. He slowly pulls out of the parking space and begins to drive west of the city.

"So where are we going? Can I ask?" I ask. We're driving away from the training facility so at this point I have no idea what's next. It would be great if we drove to a location and my family and friends jumped out announcing the greatest prank of all time.

"We have a full day. First, we have to meet with the rest of the team. I'm only 1 member of your team. There are several of us all assigned to the same person." he says.

"Why? What's so special about Angela Hamilton?" I ask.

"Nothing."

"Nothing? There's a whole team of people who've been waiting for me to show up to take the lead against this woman Angela and she's not special? Is the baby gonna grow up to be President of the United States or something? There has to be something about her that The Agency wants so bad to take her and the kids out."

"Nope. Nothing. The Agency goes through great lengths to destroy the plans that God has for any beforelife person. No one is special. If you are in your beforelife, there are probably attacks toward you all day long that you aren't even aware of. Most people don't have a clue what's really going on."

That is ridiculous. Why in the world would there be a team of people operating specifically against one woman if there wasn't something specifically important about her?

I stop asking questions as now I'm frustrated by the answers I'm getting. At least Alexander was honest with me. He realized how traumatizing this whole ordeal is so he at least told me the truth. I don't believe this Randy guy for a second. I can't fathom Angela Hamilton not being of some sort of importance if there's an entire team of us ready to take her down.

I decide to not say anything else while we drive to wherever we're going. I came to trust Alexander, Josh and Kevin. Now I'm with Randy and I don't know what I should think. I'm in his car, I don't know where I'm going and I don't know what to expect.

I break my silence when Randy pulls into the public library and finds a parking spot among the many cars already here. "The library? What are we doing here?" I ask him as he turns the engine off.

"This is where we're meeting the rest of the team. They're already here waiting on us."

"Why the library?"

"They have sound proof rooms that we use to talk. Study rooms. Come on, everyone is anxious to meet you." Randy smiles as he opens his door. I open mine and we walk into the library together.

Once inside, I scan the entire place. There are a lot of people in here but it's quiet as a mouse. Everyone is reading or using a computer. I wonder how many of these people are in the beforelife versus those working for The Agency.

My heart is racing and my palms are sweaty as I think about meeting these people. I wonder what their thoughts are about this assignment that we have. Are they as anxious and confused about it as I am? How long has each of them been waiting? How did each of them die? Still... what's the big deal about Angela Hamilton?

"Right this way." Randy says as he leads me toward a row of rooms with glass all around. The first two rooms have people in them. The third room is empty. The fourth room of the seven rooms in the row has people in it as well. Randy opens the door to the fourth room and everyone in the room stops talking and looks at us enter.

"Hey guys! Look who I have!" Randy says. This is the most excited I've heard of his voice as he says it with a gleeful smile. "Everyone, this is Brian Lampkin, our lead. Brian, this is the team. I'm gonna let everyone take a moment to introduce themselves."

"Hey... hey, wassup." I say as I nervously take one of the two empty seats. I sit next to Randy who is on my right and an African American woman on my left.

"I guess I'll start and get the introductions going." You all know me and I've already been introduced by Brian's Chief Presenter, but for the sake of getting started, hi everybody, I'm Randy!"

"Hi Randy!" another man says in a joking way which causes everyone to laugh. I smile as to join in but I still don't find any humor in any of this.

Randy continues after he chuckles. "I'm the Guidance Operative on this project. I'll be the person to answer all of your questions and help you navigate through the steps you need to take to work your assignment."

The person to Randy's right speaks next. "Hey Brian, I'm Christine, your Secondary Operative. I think I've been working for The Agency the longest out of the team because I've been here 7 years waiting for whoever the Primary Operative would be. It's nice to finally meet you."

"Nice to meet you too Christine. Please excuse me if it takes me a little while to remember all of your names." I say politely.

"No worries." she says with a smile.

"Yeah you're gonna get a complete break down of all of us tonight. I'll give you an iPad with our names, pictures and pertinent information. I'll give you that later though. You'll be able to communicate with each of us whenever you want."

"I'm Dale. I'm also a Secondary Operative."

The next guy chimes in loudly. "OK, so everybody knows I'm just as loud as I wanna be! My name is Carlos and I'm a little coo-coo!"

"A little is an understatement!" Randy says laughing. His laughter causes everyone else in the room to laugh, except me.

"That's right! I ain't ashamed to say that I hate being here, I hate all of you and Brian, I hate you too! I hate that we all in this predicament but I ain't gonna complain before one of those big security linebacker dudes shows up to drag me away! I ain't trying to go back to... that place... ever! So, pleased to meet you!" Carlos says loudly. Carlos is of Hispanic decent and speaks very loud and colorful. I can tell he had a big personality in his beforelife, whatever that was.

"You didn't even tell Brian what your role is in the assignment." Christine says.

"Oh my bad! I'm your Resource Operative!"

"Hello Brian I'm Dorothy, I'm one of our Assistant Operatives in the assignment."

"I'm JaQuita. Assistant Operative as well."

"JaQuita is probably the person closest to Angela right now so you're gonna have to stick close to her and learn a lot." Randy looks at me and says.

"So this is the team. Everyone here is specifically assigned with the same thing you are," Randy is looking at me as he speaks, "we just have different roles. So now that we've introduced ourselves, we need to take a moment to share our personal connections with the principle, Angela Hamilton. I'll start." Randy looks back in the general direction of everyone else and not so much at me. "I manage the Starbucks that Angela comes in almost every morning. I've had to make it a point to know the customers that frequent consistently on a first name basis in order for Angela to not think it strange that I know her name. When she comes in, we make small talk. I know what she wants to order. Every now and then I may give her a free pastry just because. I usually bring a smile to her face when I ask her about work or tennis." Randy turns back to me. "She went to the mall with JaQuita and I purposely ran into them. Angela's face lit up and she said my name. The purpose of me planning that interaction was to see if she knew my first name yet. She does. She introduced me to JaQuita as the nice guy who works at the Starbucks on Willingboro. JaQuita and I obviously acted as if we didn't know one another or had planned that meet up in the mall."

"So..." I'm trying to get my thoughts together. "You were hired at the Starbucks on Willingboro, specifically to meet Angela Hamilton?" I ask.

"Yeah. The Agency got me the job there and I've been there waiting on whoever would be assigned the Primary on this assignment. That Primary is you." Randy responds.

Wow. Wow.

JaQuita speaks next even though she isn't seated in the order in which the group introduced themselves. "I'm one of Angela's bff's. We do a lot of shopping together and basically just hang out. We may catch dinner and a movie or just meet for drinks. We talk all the time, almost every day."

"How did you meet Angela?" I ask.

"She had to go to a training for her job and I attended the same training. I was assigned the same line of work that she has. We met at that training. We were the only African American females in attendance so naturally, we kinda bonded. I asked her if she wanted to do lunch on the first day of the training classes and of course she said yes. We've been friends ever since."

"And how long ago was that? How long have y'all been friends?"

"I joined The Agency two years ago. Right after my orientation and training, I got my assignment and I was placed in the training program. I met her that week. So our friendship has been 2 years now."

"So wait... let me get this straight. You're telling me that members of The Agency knew Angela was going to have to go to training for her job, sent you to the training specifically to meet her," I point to JaQuita, "send you to work at her favorite coffee house," I point to Randy, "and there's nothing special about Angela? Nothing at all? Are you serious?"

There is a moment of silence in the room where everyone is staring back at me as if I said something strange. I just can't wrap my mind around the concept of this person of no importance being targeted so heavily. There must be something special about either her or her children for The Agency to put so much effort into destroying her.

"We're going to have some alone time this evening at dinner." Randy says. "I'll make sure you fully understand why all this is happening the way that it is okay?"

"Yeah. Sure."

"Don't worry, that's what I'm here for. I'm going to help guide you along to completing this assignment so any questions you have at any point, I'm your guy."

"OK."

"I'll go next!" Carlos said in his loud way. "I'm Angela's neighbor! I bought the house next to the one that she purchased last year. I know her schedule and can give you details about her week, her weekends, whatever you want bro."

"Once again I'm Dorothy. I know it may take you a little bit to remember all of our names but I'm Dorothy, one of your assistants. I work at the firm so I'm with Angela from Monday through Friday from 9 to 5. I'm the receptionist there and I do a lot of administrative work there also."

Dorothy is the only person who seems to not be OK with being here. I see concern in her face. She is the oldest person in the room by appearance but she's not an old lady by any stretch. I can tell however that this Agency experience has taken a toll on her and she, like me, would rather not be here at all.

"I'm her financial advisor." Dale says. "I help her make decisions about her money so I'm going to be a great aid to you Brian. I look forward to working with you."

"Um, same here." I say.

The final person to speak is Christine. "I'm Angela's hair stylist. She comes to the shop once every month. She may come more than once if she goes to an event for work. We talk a lot when I'm working on her hair. She opens up a lot. I'll be very helpful as your Assistant Operative also."

"And that's the team." Randy says.

"One for all and all against one right?" Carlos states with a laugh.

I slam my fist down onto the table and stand up. "I don't know what's so funny! What the hell is the matter with you?" I feel like I want to rip Carlos' head off and I just met him four minutes ago. Brian quickly stands and grabs my arm. I suppose he thinks I'm going to lunge across this table and attack Carlos. I would never do that in my beforelife. I don't suppose I would do it now. Yet, Carlos has become the straw that broke the camel's back. I've been holding this in since I learned of my assignment. I wasn't given an opportunity to digest it. I got it, I was driven here, and now I'm being introduced to a team of people that don't seem to care that our assignment is horrendous and disgusting.

"Hey man! What's the matter with you bro? Calm down okay! Sheesh!" Carlos says back to me. He stands up to back away from me. Everyone else remains seated. They all jumped when I slammed my fist down.

"Brian! Take it easy!" Randy says.

"Don't tell me to take it easy!" I forcefully push Randy's hand off me. I look up and notice that there are people in other rooms now looking our direction. I don't know who made the decision to meet in a public library in a glass room but this might not have been the best decision for our initial meeting.

"Do you want to go back to Hell forever? Do you?" Randy's question gets my attention immediately. I look at him and find myself speechless. "I didn't think so! Look! We don't want to go back to Hell either but that all depends on you! You know what's at stake! You just finished all that training!

Don't blow this man! Come on! Focus!"

I slowly sit down. Carlos sits too.

"You know what, let's call it a day for now. I think the introductions are enough for one day. You all have to keep in mind that we've been waiting for Brian for a long time but Brian just learned of his assignment today. We've all had time to think hard about what this means. He hasn't."

"Yes. You're absolutely right." Dorothy says softly.

"Y'all go back to your regularly scheduled daily activities and I'll communicate back with you in let's say... two days." Randy says.

"Meeting adjourned I guess! Adios!" Carlos says proudly. "I don't know about you all, I'm going to eat!"

With Carlos' declaration, everyone stands to leave. I remain seated as does Randy. Everyone leaves after saying goodbye to me. Randy and I remain seated. Dale is the last person to leave the room and he closes the glass door behind himself. Randy and I remain in the room.

"Don't worry about Carlos. He was silly in his beforelife. He's sillier now. We all have ways of coping with the afterlife and working for the Agency. This is just his way to cope."

"Yeah. Okay."

I don't believe Randy knows what to say next. Neither do I. We sit in silence. Two men, already dead yet living. He finally breaks the silence with something that will make me feel a little better. "I know you're hungry. Let me take you home. You need to get some sleep. We got a lot to do tomorrow."

"I'm almost afraid to ask what tomorrow has in store." I

say as we stand.

"Tomorrow will be a much better day. We pick up your new vehicle tomorrow."

"I... I get a new vehicle?"

"Yeah. We have to go to the dealership to pick it up. Silver Lexus LS 460."

For the first time, I wake up without having to go to a training class. I don't have Josh or Kevin waiting for me to go crazy. I don't have Alexander picking me up. Instead, Randy said he would be here at 8:00 to take me to get my new car and cell phone. This is Day 1 of my assignment.

As expected, Randy is on time. He pulls up in front of my place at exactly 8:00. I've learned that members of The Agency respect time far more than people in the beforelife. We on this side understand how precious time is and that we are on limited time.

"Sleep well?" he asks as I enter his car.

"Yeah. Another great dinner and I tried to relax my mind. Watched the game too." I say as I fasten my seat belt.

"Good. Our appointment at the dealership isn't until 10:00 but I wanted to meet you at 8:00 to take you to breakfast. We have a lot to discuss and get you ready for."

"Okay."

"Any questions you got for me so far? I know there must be a ton of questions on your mind." Randy says as we drive toward the outskirts of town. The only breakfast spot out there is IHOP, which is fine with me.

"Yeah. I don't even know where to begin. I got so many questions."

"Well let's start at the very beginning and work our way up. Let me tell you about myself and then we'll get into where you and I fit together. Um, my name in my beforelife was Scott McGregor. I died very young. I had a very rare lung disease called Idiopathic Pulmonary Fibrosis. I know you don't know what that means. The only reason I know is because I had been dealing with it and going to treatments almost all my life. It finally took me out."

"Nah, I never heard of that." I say.

"Yeah, so that did it for me. Next thing I know, I'm screaming like crazy and then I had a Chief Presenter talking real calm to me. I thought I was dreaming. You know the rest."

"So why did they assign you to work at Starbucks?"

"In my beforelife I was a retail store manager. I always go along well with customers and coworkers. My assignment is to get close to the principle and help you get close to her too. As long as she trusts me, even from a distance, I'll be helping you more than you'll ever realize."

"Wow."

"Yeah. So that's how I got to be this part of the assignment. Each person has their own story and you'll get to hear from them each. They can tell you how they died and came into their particular part of the assignment."

"Okay..."

"I know a major question is how you got to your part of the assignment."

"Yes!" This is the question that has been on my mind the strongest. Why? And why me?

"In your beforelife, you were a powerful marketing executive. You commanded attention and made things happen for your firm. People admired you and looked up to you. Your afterlife will be the same. You're a powerful executive in a marketing firm again. That's why you're being set up in a Lexus. Top of the line."

"I'm gonna have a job in marketing?"

"Yes. You're very good. That's why your place is set up very similar to what you had before. Your clothes are what you would have already picked out for yourself. The food prepared for you is top notch. Better than what I get. They replicated your beforelife to help you with your assignment in your afterlife. It's all done on purpose."

I'm speechless for a moment. I honestly don't know what to say. The more I learn, the more I am horrified and impressed.

"You know, I assumed that all members of The Agency were being fed like I'm being fed. The lunch is outstanding so I assumed all the food was like that." I say.

"I wish! The lunch is outstanding for new inductees. After training, you settle in to ordinary life, just working an assignment. I tell you what, I know I would be at your place a lot to eat dinner but that would mess up your assignment. It would be a little difficult to explain to Angela why the Starbucks guy keeps stopping by for lobster and steak."

We arrive at IHOP and are seated. "Okay, so I'm a marketing executive. What does Angela do?" I ask.

"Glad you asked." Randy reaches into his backpack and pulls out an iPad. He turns it on and places it on the table in front of me. "Here's her entire portfolio. Angela works for Pittman right downtown."

"The law Firm?" I ask as I look at her photo. She is gorgeous.

"Yeah. She's a corporate attorney and an adjunct professor. You can read it all if you click the Bio button on the right." Randy picks up the IHOP menu just as the waitress comes over to introduce herself. I ignore her and look at Angela's picture again. She's beautiful. I guess The Agency knows the type of woman I would be interested in dating because if I ever saw Angela in my beforelife, I would definitely ask her out. She looks like she works out and is on top of her game. She is dressed in a business suit with a no nonsense look on her face. Her arms are folded but in a non-aggressive way. She looks like she means business. Her hair and make-up are impeccable. I already feel challenged just knowing I must somehow cause her to fall for me.

"And for you sir?" The waitress taps her pad with her pen to get my attention.

"Oh... um..."

"He'll have a large orange juice, no ice." Randy orders exactly what I would have ordered for myself. I almost ask him how he knew but The Agency studied me of course.

The waitress walks away and we resume talking. "As you can see, Angela is no slouch herself. She's a perfect match for you. She's head strong, confident, intelligent and beautiful." Randy says. "You're gonna have your work cut out for you."

I don't respond. I continue to look at her bio. Originally from New Jersey, undergraduate degree from Rutgers University. Masters degree from Columbia University. Law degree from Howard University. Began her career at The Law Offices of Schuman, Jones and Jurkowski. From there, she made a career move to The Pittman Law Firm. She has been with Pittman for 7 years.

"A woman like this I would think would already be married. She doesn't have a serious boyfriend or anything?" I ask.

"No. She's never been married. She doesn't have children. Deep down that's what she wants though. Just like a lot of women, she wants the knight in shining armor to show up. The problem is that she's been hurt. Her last relationship took a lot out of her and she's closed off to love right now."

"What happened with the last guy?" Our drinks arrive just as I ask.

"Are you guys ready to order?"

"Uh yeah. Let me get the breakfast scrambler with toast and extra bacon." Randy says.

"Okay. And you sir?" The waitress turns to me. I haven't even looked at the menu.

"Yeah I'll get the same thing he's getting."

"No problem." She grabs our menus and walks away.

"She was with a guy named Rob for two years. She let her guard down and fell madly in love with him. As far as she was concerned, she was ready to walk down the aisle. He's a fitness instructor. He has a ton of clients that he works out with and teaches them healthy habits. Angela caught him cheating with one of his clients. It broke her heart."

"Wow, that's tough."

"She took it very hard. You're fighting an uphill battle with that. She won't be jumping all over you once you start to woo her. I can guarantee you that!" Randy smiles as he picks up his glass of water and takes a sip.

"Have you all worked out how I'm supposed to meet her?" I ask. "Do I just run into her in the club or something?"

Randy laughs. "Funny. No. Your company was in the bidding for a contract and another firm got the job. Your company filed a complaint that they were discriminated against in the honoring of the contract. The Pittman Firm is taking the case. You're going to meet her in one of the meetings between your job and hers."

The Agency is amazing! I can't believe this!

"And once again, there's nothing special about Angela Hamilton? All of this effort, planning, secret and divisive activity is just because?" I ask.

"Angela Hamilton is no more special than Wendy." Randy replies.

"Who is Wendy?"

"Our waitress bringing our food right now."

During our chat at breakfast, I learned that the marketing firm that I work for is called The Paradigm Group. They gave me a corner office with a nice view of the city. I have a flat screen TV and a sitting area in my office. The office I have now is very similar to the office I had in my beforelife. The Agency truly goes through great lengths to execute what they do. I'm still amazed daily as I learn new things about my afterlife. As amazed as I am, I'm equally horrified with the life I have to live and the assignment I have to perform. As horrendous as it is, it's not nearly as bad as the alternative.

Before the sun rises today, I'm already dressed and out the door. Today is my first day driving on my own and the more I thought about it, the more I didn't want to sit in traffic. I fear seeing someone from my beforelife driving in the car next to me. They won't recognize me but I will certainly recognize them. I don't know if I'm ready for that yet. I'd rather leave early and come home late. I also want to get used to my new car.

Randy and I went to the Lexus dealership for our appointment and picked up my new car. The terms were favorable based on my income. We went through all the motions as if I was walking in and buying a car in my beforelife. When it comes to vehicles, I may have gotten an upgrade from my beforelife to my afterlife.

After picking up my car and new cell phone, I spent the evening alone in my place. I ate another great meal and played with my new phone. I thought about all that today would entail. I'm starting a new job that I never applied for. I'm qualified but don't want the job. It's the job behind the job that frightens me to tears. The consequence of not performing my job however dries my tears and puts my poker face back.

My impression of Randy changed after spending most of the day with him. Upon meeting him, I was expecting another Alexander. He's not like Alexander at all. I began to realize that there are two reasons he and Alexander differ. First, they are just different people. More importantly though, Alexander is a Chief Presenter. He is a guide. He is a role model and mentor. It's who he is and was his purpose. He is designed to help people and guide them through situations. Randy on the other hand is a manager. He has a certain level of control over the group working with me and his 9-5 job is managing a coffee shop. Once I recognized that he wouldn't serve as a mentor, I lowered my expectations in that regard. He did his best to answer my questions and he was sincere in all his answers. I can appreciate that for what it's worth.

As I pull up to the office to my new job, I survey the building, the outside and the surrounding area. I've never spent time on this part of town so the chances of me running into someone I know is probably slim. The Agency thought of everything! They acquired a job for me in a part of town that I would probably be safe from seeing someone that I know and at the same time a job that will cause me to interact with the principal of my assignment.

I'm early so I stay in my new car and listen to the morning show on the radio. My new phone vibrates and I'm immediately surprised. No one has this number. I'm almost afraid to answer it. I look and instantly calm down as I see the only name I put in the phone so far... Randy.

"Have a good first day of work today. Talk to you later."

I text back. "Thanks."

I put the phone down and lay my head back. I close my eyes. I remember my first day at my former job in my beforelife and try to imagine it being similar to what I'm walking into today. I guess I'm about to find out.

"Brian! Listen man, I'm sorry I wasn't available to join the conference call with the hiring manager but welcome to our team! I hope you're ready to get to work because you're gonna get a lot of projects piled up on your desk!" A well dressed man in an expensive French cuff shirt with sparkling cuff links extends his hand toward me. This must be Reggie. His real name is Corey but he goes by his middle name. Randy downloaded a chart of everyone here at The Paradigm Group or TPG as they like to call themselves, and of everyone on my team with The Agency.

"Nice to finally meet you man. I'm excited to be here." I say as I take his hand. I look him directly in his eye and try to break his hand with the tightest squeeze I can give. I learned how important initial interactions are when I was in my beforelife. I always shook another man's hand with authority. My confidence is the first thing I want a client or partner to learn about me.

"Let me show you to your new digs. Don't know if Shay told you but we got a conference call in 40 minutes." Shay is his personal assistant. Randy showed me a group of email correspondences she sent me to get me acclimated to my career here. "So don't get too settled in. Put your stuff down and then we can do the call from my office."

"Okay, that works." I respond.

Reggie introduces me to the other employees as he walks me to my office. Everyone smiles and says "Hello." Some say "Welcome to the team." One female employee looks me up and down and smiles as if she's interested in getting to know me after hours. I quickly notice her wedding ring and I laugh to myself. Reggie opens my office for me and stands aside so I can enter the room.

"You got 40 minutes. My office is down the hall on the right. You can't miss it. I'll leave the door open for you."

"Thanks man. I'll be right there." I say as I take off my suit jacket and lay it neatly over the arm of my office couch. I walk to the large window that overlooks this part of my city that I'm not as familiar with. I take a moment to breathe it all in. As I turn around, I look at the flat screen TV, the glass desk, the book shelf, and the couch set in my new office. All of this to meet Angela Hamilton.

A man peeks his head into my office and knocks on the door. "Brian?"

"Yeah, that's me." I respond.

The young man steps in smiling. He's a lot younger than I am. He reminds me of the intern I was texting when this horrible nightmare began. "I'm Eric. Just wanted to pop in to say what's up."

"Yeah, Eric. I saw your name on the company flow chart. You're the whiz kid out of Ivy League right?"

Eric laughs. "I don't know if I would say whiz kid. I did well in school."

"Man, that's an understatement. You got a bright future ahead. Good to meet you. If you ever need anything, let me know. I remember when I started my career and I had somebody at my old firm that took me under his wing. That helped me a lot so I can do the same for you."

Eric smiles an even bigger smile than when he walked in. "Man, that would be great! Thanks! I appreciate that!"

"No problem young man, good to meet you. Looking forward to tackling some projects with you." I pat Eric on the shoulder and shake his hand.

"Yes sir!" he says excitedly.

"Are you in on this call with Reggie too?" I ask.

"No. I'm already on another project so I gotta run but just wanted to officially meet you. I don't get a fancy office like you so I'll be in one of those cubicles out there." He points to the common area where a lot of the workers are in cubicles.

"Don't let your goal be an office like this. Let your goal be owning a business where you can afford to give out offices like this." I say. My statement causes Eric to smile again. He seems to smile a lot and that may take him far. He seems to have a positive outlook. As he leaves, I grab my portfolio and make my way to Reggie's office for the conference call. Like showing up at work, I want to show up for the call early as well.

Reggie's office is similar to mine, just opposite since it's on the other side of the hall. He's already on the phone so I knock before I step inside. He looks up and waves me in. I sit in one of the chairs in front of his desk. Reggie talks for another 5 minutes before he finishes his call. He then calls Shay to come in to his office.

"So we're off and running. We have a few things to discuss on the call and the first two things are pretty big." Reggie says to me.

"Okay, I'm ready." I respond.

"As soon as Shay comes in I'm gonna..." As Reggie is speaking, Shay walks into the room holding a pen and pad. "Oh hey, speak of the devil. I was just about to say I'm gonna dial in to the call line as soon as you come in."

I don't like the word devil anymore. Makes me uncomfortable.

Reggie introduced me to his assistant Shay a few minutes ago. She seems very attentive to Reggie as she was giving him details as he introduced me to her. Although she smiled and spoke to me, she began telling Reggie about the call we're calling into now and a few meetings he has scheduled for this afternoon.

Reggie dials into the conference call line and puts the call on speaker. He asks Shay to close his door, but I get up and close it for him.

"Good afternoon, this is Reggie Ward and Brian Lampkin from TPG on the call. Got Shay Saunders here as well. Is anyone on the call yet?" Reggie says into the speaker.

"Hey Mr. Ward, thanks for calling in and bringing us in on this case. This is Joe Taylor and with me on the call I have attorneys Bob Crandall and Angela Hamilton."

My phone rings as soon as I put my key into the lock to open my door. I quickly open the door and drop my portfolio onto my counter. "Hello?"

"Hey man! It's Carlos!"

"Oh, what's up man. I need to save your number in my phone." I say as I turn my lights on.

"Yeah man, Randy just gave me your number. Just wanted to check in on you bro. How did your first day go today?" Carlos is just as loud on the phone as he is in person.

"Went well. I jumped right in when I got there. They waste no time in getting their new executives busy. First call of the morning and I heard Angela's voice."

"Did you? Your future wife! Wow, that was fast! First day! I thought it might be sometime this week!" he says surprised.

"Well I still haven't met her but just to hear her voice gave me chills. Like seriously. I wasn't ready."

"I understand totally! When I first got my assignment, I had no idea how I was gonna even play a part in this! Then, they tell me that they bought a house with furniture and I had to move in right next door to her! How crazy is that bro? So, I just rolled with it of course and then I met her. It was surreal! Like, really weird!"

"What's she really like?" I ask. I've read the bio that The Agency has put together on her but I'd really like to hear personal accounts from Carlos and JaQuita specifically. They probably know her personality the best out of everyone on the team. The Agency compiled statistics. I have her birthday, her favorite color, favorite restaurant, some of her likes and dislikes. I know she likes to read and watch superhero movies. Her bio reads like an online dating bio.

"She's a tough cookie. She's no nonsense. I think your biggest challenge bro is gonna be breaking through her shell. Once you do, you gonna be okay. You have to. Lean on the team. That's what we here for. We're gonna work together to get our assignment done. I'm not goin' back bro. I'm not goin' back!"

Dinner tonight is avocado salsa chicken sprinkled with monterey jack cheese and mild salsa. I grab my plate and opt for a soda tonight. Not in a wine mood. I plop down on the couch with my plate in one hand, my iPad in the other, and my bottle of Sprite under my arm. I turn the TV on and wait for it to boot up. I haven't decided whether I want to watch basketball or something on Netflix. In the meantime, I pull up Angela's profile on my iPad.

Angela Hamilton is a beautiful woman with a lot going for herself. She is an established attorney at a prestigious firm. She owns a home in a nice neighborhood. She doesn't have to answer to anyone. She is totally independent and has been that way for some time.

I can tell by reading a little about her where she gets her tough exterior from. Her parents divorced when she was very young. Her father only maintained contact for the first few years. Her mother had a nervous breakdown and relinquished custody of Angela to her best friend. Angela confided in JaQuita that she finds it impossible to trust men after what her father and last boyfriend did... walked out on her.

I take a moment to let that sink in. This woman has her heart broken several times over the course of her life. She is now at a place where she won't trust a man because experience tells her that trusting men will leave her shattered and broken. Its now my job to convince her to open her heart again so that I can shatter and break it. I've never imagined deception like this was even possible, let alone, I would play a part in something so dastardly.

In this moment, I feel horrible for Angela. She doesn't deserve what I'm assigned to do to her. Our children would be innocent. Our grandchildren would be innocent. She is innocent. What is being plotted against her is the worst crime ever committed in the history of mankind. My heart aches for her and I feel myself being overcome with emotion. As tears build up in my eyes, I look up at my ceiling so the tears will flow back into my eyes and not down my cheeks.

Angela... my son... my daughter... my children... my family...

I remember the look of determination the demon in my last dream had when he came after me. He grabbed me and threw me to the ground like I weighed two pounds. I remember how the ground was burning and how both my legs were on fire. I remember so many people screaming in pain and falling over one another. I remember falling into the lake and going under. The heat was so excruciating that I opened my mouth to scream but the boiling lava-like liquid poured down my throat. I remember my face and hands being on fire. I remember the screams and the stench.

I rub my temples and place my iPad down next to me on the couch. I pick up the remote control and scroll through Netflix until I find House of Cards. I pick up my plate and begin eating one of the best chicken dishes I've ever had.

"Good morning Shay. How you doing this morning?" I ask with a smile?

"I'm good, thanks for asking. How are you?"

"Awesome." I reply. I say Hello to a few more people as I walk into my office. I sit down behind my desk and take out my work tablet. As I login to respond to an email from yesterday, my phone rings. I look at the phone and see that Dorothy is calling me. I quickly stand up and walk to the open door of my office and close it. I then answer the phone.

"Hello?"

"Hi Brian, it's Dorothy."

"Um, hi. Is everything okay?" I ask in a very reserved tone.

"Oh yes, everything is fine. I'm sorry if I startled you by calling. I didn't mean to do that. I was just calling to say Hello and wish you a good day." she says.

My heart had begun to race when I saw Dorothy's name on my phone. Seeing her name immediately threw me into panic mode as I thought something bad had happened within our assignment.

"You scared the crap out of me! Man, I thought something was wrong!" I say with a huge laugh. I don't want Dorothy to feel bad about calling me to say hello. She is an older woman and reminds me of Frank from my training class.

"I'm so sorry. I didn't mean to frighten you."

"It's okay, no problem. I appreciate you calling in."

"It's slow over here at the office. I usually just sit here and read a magazine. In about 30 minutes, I'll be a lot busier as calls begin to come in for the lawyers. I set up the conference room for meetings and... hold please." I can hear her speaking to someone as she doesn't put me on hold. "Yes, I will have that ready for you in about an hour. Yes Sir. Okay." She comes back to me. "Brian?"

"Yeah I'm here."

"Sorry about that. So yeah, I set up the conference room for meetings and do a lot of busy work."

"How often do you see Angela?" I ask.

"Every day unless she's in court. She always smiles at me and says hello. She gave me a card last year for Mother's Day which I thought was very nice."

"You have children?" I ask.

She laughs before she answers. "No, well not in the afterlife. In the beforelife I did. But she thinks I have children because I have a picture of grandchildren on my desk. They aren't my actual children, just a prop provided for me by The Agency."

These people have thought of everything. "Wow, I would've never thought of that. The Agency is so detailed."

"Yes indeed. The Agency leaves no stone unturned, that's for sure." Dorothy says.

There's an awkward silence before Dorothy speaks again. "Brian I know this assignment seems horrible but trust me, you can do this. We're all counting on you."

"I'm sure you are. We all get deported if I fail right?" I ask already knowing her answer.

"Yes but let's not discuss failure. I tend to focus on being here and not being there okay?"

"Yes Ma'am." Dorothy seems like somebody's sweet grandmother. Her being in this predicament is mind boggling. I now see people in an entire different light. I may have passed one million Dorothys in my travels and never would have thought that they were working for The Agency and doomed just like I am. She smiles as a receptionist but is dying inside... dying to live.

I hear a knock on my door.

"Hey, somebody is at my door so I gotta go."

"Okay, Brian. Have a good day okay? Stay focused." Dorothy says.

"I will. You too." I end the call. "Come in, it's not locked." My door opens and Eric peeks his head in.

"Hey bro! You busy? I saw your door closed." He says.

"Nah man, I'm good. Come on in." Eric steps in with a smile. "You got weekend plans? Saturday!"

"Not that I know of. Why? Wassup?" I ask.

Eric whips his hand from around his back. I hadn't even noticed that he had his hand behind his back. "Look what I got! Two tickets! Saturday night! Clifton Burgess is comin' to town and I got two tickets! Down front! Not courtside but good seats!"

"Are you serious?" I say loudly. I literally jump out of my chair and come around my desk to where Eric is standing. He puts the two tickets in my hand and sure enough, they are legitimate NBA tickets. I can't believe it. I was a big fan of Clifton Burgess in my beforelife and I've never seen him play in person. This is awesome.

"Yeah man! I'm serious! Believe it or not, I won a radio contest like a month ago! I actually forgot about it and then boom! Got these tickets in the mail last night! So I thought it would be cool to see if you wanted to go. Kinda like a guys night out to get to know one another. You in?"

"Most definitely! Thanks man! Wow, I really appreciate that! I'm surprised you invited me but I definitely wanna go!" I say in an excited tone. I haven't taken my eyes off the tickets since I grabbed them.

"My lady isn't into sports. I told her I won the tickets and you would've thought I said I was taking out the trash. No big deal to her. One of my boys from college would probably want to go but his mom has been sick and he really hasn't left her side. I don't think she's doing well." Eric says.

"Oh man, I'm sorry to hear that for your friend."

"Yeah. Thanks. I knew he wouldn't be able to go so I thought about you. I thought it would be a great way to kinda get to know you. I wasn't sure if you were into basketball but if you are, we can go."

"Well I will absolutely take you up on your offer. Thanks a lot!"

"Cool! Aight, let me go act like I work here. Talk to ya later!" Eric takes the tickets back and walks toward my door. "You want me to close this?"

"No, you can leave it open. Thanks."

Eric walks out, leaving my office door open. I pick up my tablet from my desk and walk toward the couch in my office. Sitting down, I open my email folder to see what I have on my to do list for the day. I'm not sure if it's The Agency or this job itself but I have a full list of things according to my email. There are several projects that I need to make phone calls for and introduce myself. In my beforelife, I was very involved with all my firm's clients. This will have to be the same if I am to focus on my task.

The basketball game will be a nice distraction. I can't wait.

"Hey Brian!" I look up from my tablet and see Reggie standing at the door of my office.

"Morning."

"Breaking news. If you saw the email about the conference call at 10:00, that's cancelled. They're coming here instead."

"I didn't see the email yet. I just logged in. Who is coming here?"

"The lawyers. The Pittman law group. They want to do a face-to-face instead of a call today so they're on their way over. Do you need to get briefed? I know we're kinda throwing you into this thing suddenly, but I want you in there with me if you think you're ready." Reggie says.

Reggie is asking me if I'm prepared to present our firm's case to the law firm representing us. I'm much more concerned that today is the day I meet Angela. I'm not prepared for either but I have no other options.

"Yeah, I'm good. I read the entire complaint and I'm sure they just want to put a face with a name today. They're probably going to walk us through the process and answer any questions we have. It's not a big deal." I say. I'm trying to speak calmly but I can feel every beat of my heart in my brain, my throat and my chest. "I'll be fine."

"Good. Come down to the lobby in about 40 or 45 minutes and we can meet them when they come in." Reggie says as he turns to leave my office.

"Okay man. Thanks for the heads up. Can you close my door?"

Reggie closes my door and I immediately stand up from the couch and walk quickly to my desk. I grab my phone and see that I missed a call and four text messages. Dorothy called back. I open the texts and see that it is a group text from everyone on my team. Dorothy started it just to let me and everyone else know that Angela is on her way to my office. Christine, Dale and Randy each say good luck. Dorothy texts one word... focus!

To say that I'm now nervous is an understatement. I'm about to meet the woman of my dreams and my nightmares. In my heart, I don't want to go through with this but in my mind, I have to. The alternative is far worse than what I'm about to do. I've already told my heart that it has to sit this life out and be controlled by my mind. Every time I think about the lake of fire, the demons, the smell and the incredible burning fire, I'm ready to complete my assignment.

I send a text to JaQuita. "I'm about to meet her. Give me one word of advice."

I sit down behind my desk and put my phone down. I cover my face with both of my hands.

In my beforelife, I made one huge error at work. It was the only time I had ever made a major mistake in my career. I jeopardized an account that had been with our team for over 10 years. When it seemed as if we would lose the account, I knew I would be fired. I knew my name would be mud all over town and in every agency. I wouldn't be able to find a job in my industry. Once your name is out and your blackballed, you can forget about it. The account was a little short of one million dollars and our firm would take a huge hit if we lost that account due to incompetence. I remember now sitting in my office then in the same position I am now. Elbows on my desk with my palms covering my face. I didn't want to take my hands down to face what was about to happen. I built my career on my own confidence and ability to be tough in difficult situations. In that moment however, I was afraid. I was at the mercy of someone else and I had no control over what the outcome would be. I had no relief as I stared down the tunnel of uncertainty. I hated that feeling in my beforelife. I hate that feeling now in my afterlife. I don't want to take my hands down and face the fact that in minutes, I'm going to meet the woman whose life I'm now destined to destroy.

My phone vibrates which brings my hands down from in front of my face. It's a text message from JaQuita. "Stay calm. Don't ask her out. Don't be aggressive. Just be yourself and talk about your case with her firm. I'll find out what she thinks of you and report back to the group. Good luck!"

Reggie and I step aside to allow Shay to step on the elevator first. She presses the button for the first floor. I feel like that stepping onto the elevator and the motion going downward are all in slow motion.

"I heard you got tickets to the game you lucky bastard!" Reggie says to me with a smile on his face.

"Huh?" I'm still in a trance and his statement snaps me out of it. I'm glad he snapped me out because I don't need to be in a trance when I meet Angela.

"Eric. I heard he got tickets to the game and he gave one to you. Monica told me."

"Oh yeah! Dude, I was just as shocked as you! But I know one thing... I'm goin'!" I quickly change my attitude and join in on the fun. Both Reggie and Shay laugh as the elevator arrives on the lobby level of our building. We again step aside to allow Shay to walk out first.

Angela is wearing a dark blue business suit with a white shirt. Her pictures do her little justice as she is more beautiful in person. She has definitely accessorized her outfit well with the accompanying bracelet and shoes. I'm big on accessories myself so I notice them on other people. Angela and I would do well in an exclusive designer specialty boutique.

Of her team of three, she is the only one seated in one of our lobby chairs. Her partners, Joe Taylor and Bob Crandall are standing.

Reggie leads the way and as he approaches, Angela stands. "Gentlemen and lady, thank you for adjusting your schedule and coming on such short notice. I'm Reggie." Reggie shakes the first man's hand.

"Reggie, I'm Bob. This is obviously Angela, and this is

Joe."

"Angela... Bob." Reggie says as he shakes their hands in order.

For the next five seconds, we shake hands. I approach Angela after I greet Joe and Bob. "Good morning, I'm Brian." I say. I don't smile at her as to keep a professional appearance, but I purposely look directly into her eyes to see if she turns away. She doesn't. Angela is confident, and I like that in person.

"Hello Brian, nice to finally put some faces with these names." She says with a smile.

We walk back to the elevator and I can hear my heart thumping in my chest. I take a few deep breaths and try not to seem so conspicuous. I remember in high school when I would try to cheat on an exam. I feel like everyone in the classroom was staring at me for the entire duration of the test. Every time I made a move to look at the prewritten answers in my hand, all eyes were on me. Everyone seemed to know my intent and was just waiting on the moment that I looked at my answers. Once I did, they were going to bust me. I now feel as if everyone in this elevator is looking at me and knowing my cruel intentions with Angela.

I watch Angela from the side of my eye as we enter the conference room. She's an attorney's attorney. I can already tell that she's about her business and no nonsense.

"Lady and gentlemen, thank you so much for taking the time to hear our case. We definitely feel that we have a legitimate case in the awarding of this contract and didn't hesitate to reach out to who we felt was the best firm to handle this." Reggie opens the discussion after taking his seat last. He closed the door once everyone had entered and sits at the head of the table. I am sitting between Joe and Shay. Angela is across the table from me.

"When Joe told me about your company's situation, I immediately wanted to work on the case with him. We felt Angela would be a perfect fit as she has the energy and experience to deal with a case like this," Bob says.

"I've dealt with two other cases like this. I appreciate Joe trusting me enough to work with me and you guys for reaching out to us. From what I understand, there was definitely bias in the awarding of the contract and we can dig deep into what happened and try to rectify the situation." For the first time I hear Angela speak. Although she said hello and I heard her voice, now I really hear her voice. She is passionate about her career and in a few short sentences, I can tell that she means business.

At this exact moment, I remember what I'm here for. I remember the burn. I remember the heat. I remember the lake of fire. I remember all the screaming people. I remember the angel turned demon that looked like he wanted to tear me in half. I remember the smell. I remember falling onto a burning ground. I remember the man who shoved me as he was trying to get away from a demon. I remember being thrown like I weighed nothing. I remember a woman screaming at the top of her lungs for someone to help her. I remember the liquid lava on my face. I remember looking at both of my hands and they were on fire.

I close my eyes for a moment to remind myself that I can do this. I encourage myself to detach any emotion I may begin to feel for her or her children. I can do this. I have to do this. I'm not going back to Hell one second before I am forced to. If that is twenty thousand years from now and it takes me taking down Angela and her children to do so... so be it.

I enter the library and know exactly where to go. I'm right on time for the meeting and am extremely curious as to what the next steps are. Now that I've formally met Angela, where do I go from here? As I approach the glass study rooms, I see that everyone is here except Christine. I enter the room and take my seat.

"Hey everybody." I say.

"What's up Champ! How you feelin'?" Carlos says.

"I'm OK. I could complain but for what right?" I respond.

"Listen, I don't wanna hear no complaints no how! So yeah. Keep that to yourself and let's keep it moving!" Carlos smiles as he says what he says.

"So you met Angela and we need to discuss how that all went. I also have some info on what the next phase is going to be." Randy says in a much more serious tone than Carlos.

"Okay."

"First, we want to all say congratulations on successfully meeting her. You showed a lot of poise in sitting through that meeting. You kept your composure and for that you deserve applause. We won't clap for you here in the library but just know you did well." Randy says.

"Proud of you." Dorothy says like she is my auntie congratulating me on finishing high school.

"What are your first impressions of her?" Dale asks me.

"She's serious. Of course, I've only seen her in a business setting but she's not playing around. She knows her stuff and I can tell she's a beast in the courtroom. I wouldn't want to go up against her. Now, I'm curious to see if she's always so serious or if she lets her hair down when she's out of the workplace."

"She definitely lets her hair down." JaQuita says. "She likes to act silly and jump around just like anybody else. You'll never see that when she's at work. We went to my company's Christmas party last year and danced like nobody was watching. Then the next Monday, she was back in court and I was back at my desk as a professional. She can turn it on and off just like I can."

"That's good to know." I say.

Just as I say that, Christine opens the door and walks in. "Sorry I'm late guys. My last appointment arrived at the salon late. It pushed my time back an hour and a half."

"It's fine." Randy says. "We were just hearing Brian's first impression of Angela."

Christine smiles as she sits down. "So what you think? Serious huh?" Christine asks.

"Definitely. Most definitely." I respond.

"Okay, great. Once again, glad your first impression and initial meeting went well Brian." Randy says.

"Just remember, keep your focus and keep it professional. Don't loosen up until you start dating and even then, stay focused." Dale says. Dale seems to be a gentleman of few words. He is the opposite of Carlos. I don't know if that was done by design by The Agency but they have put together a unique team. Dorothy who seems like everyone's favorite aunt. Carlos is the obnoxious comedian. Randy, the coffee maker who manages the java and the team. Christine, who keeps the hair stunning and professional. JaQuita, who seems street savvy but professional in her own right. Dale, the quiet business man who understands the numbers.

Throw me in the mix and we have quite a crew.

"JaQuita has the next phase. I believe you said you received it this morning?" Randy says while motioning for JaQuita to speak.

"Yes." JaQuita picks up her phone and pulls something up. She begins to speak while looking at her phone. "Okay, so the next phase is to meet in a less business environment, so they want us to run into each other at Café Ekemaj on the other side of town."

"Wow, so The Agency is setting up my next meeting with Angela. "I've been there before. Nice spot." I say.

"There's a speed dating event there on Saturday. I'm dragging Angela out of the house to go and you're going to be there as well." JaQuita says.

"Speed dating?" I ask. I hate those types of events.

"It makes sense if you think about it, bro." Carlos interrupts. "You just met Angela so when she comes into the event and sees you, that's your ice breaker! You can be like 'Hey, Angela from the office! I'm Brian remember?' That can be your intro."

"That is exactly your intro." JaQuita continues. "I'm gong to act like I don't know you of course. You will wind up at each other's table and recognize one another from the case. Then, when the event is over, you two will sit alone and strike up a conversation. I'll leave you two alone to talk while I step away. After the event, I'll tell her how handsome you are and how charming you seemed and blah blah blah. Then whatever she says about you I'll relay to the team through our Group Me."

"That should work well." Dorothy says.

"Yeah, that's a great plan." Randy says.

One by one, everyone comments and agrees that this meetup idea with Angela is going to work for Saturday night. I agree. It's a solid plan and I'm ready.

I've gone from being overly anxious about finding out what my assignment is to becoming overly anxious to work my assignment. This interactive assignment is beyond terrible but I'm going to complete it because Hell is far more terrible than this assignment.

As soon as I put my key into the door of my office, I hear my name and turn around. Eric is approaching me smiling.

"Good morning Sir." I say to greet him.

"Hey man! You ready for tomorrow night?" he says. "I was thinking we could meet up at Giorgio's before the game and get some wings and beer. I don't want to pay the prices for wings at the arena. They charge an arm, a leg, and four toes just for 6 buffalo wings!" Eric says laughing.

Dammit the game! "Oh crap! The game! Dude! I totally forgot that we got tickets to the game tomorrow night and something came up that I can't miss! Ah man! How could I have forgotten about the game! Damn! I'm sorry man, I can't go!" Eric is looking at me as if I just slapped his beloved mother. He looks heartbroken that I have to cancel our plans. I became so focused on the speed dating event that I totally forgot about the game. As much as I would love to see Clifton Burgess play, there's no way I can miss an appointment that has to do with my assignment. "Man I'm so sorry!"

"Wow... so I see you bought their entire story huh?" Eric says.

"Huh?" I respond.

"The Agency. You actually believe everything they tell you?"

"What?" Eric's words hit me like a freight train. How does he know about The Agency?

Eric slowly turns around and closes my door. He lowers his voice as he continues. "Those guys at The Agency told you that you're destined to go to Hell and you believed every word they said. Really dude? If they told you that the moon was made of green cheese would you believe that too?"

My mouth is wide open and I don't know what to say. I feel like I'm about to pass out. I try to push words out of my mouth to respond but nothing audible exits my mouth. I'm literally speechless. Of the countless things I could say, the best I can come up with is a question. "So... you're a member of The Agency too?"

"No... not anymore!" Eric says with a serious look. "I got out of The Agency 3 years ago!"

"You got out? I thought there was no way to get out!" I say at almost a scream.

"Lower your voice!" Eric says.

"How can I get out!" I grab Eric's arm almost in desperation. If he was a member of The Agency and was able to get out, then I need to find out what he did. If everything I've been told is a lie, I need to find that out too. I took Alexander's word for everything he said. The pain I felt was real, the dreams were real. Everything seemed so real. Maybe he left a part out. Maybe he didn't tell me that there is a way out. Maybe I can avoid going to Hell forever.

"Hey man! Calm down!" Eric snatches his arm away from me and as soon as he does I violently grab him again.

"Eric help me get out! Help me man!" I scream and shake him.

"Len! Calm down man! They got cameras in here!"

"What?" I let go of his arm and frantically look around the room like I'm scanning for cameras. "How do you know my real name?"

"Listen, meet me at Giorgio's tonight after work and I'll explain the whole thing." Eric responds. He never answers the question about my name. He acts as if he didn't hear it.

"No! You're going to tell me right now!" my voice is still raised as I'm desperately seeking answers.

"Len! The Agency is watching! We can't talk here!" Eric whispers. He then pauses and looks around as if there was someone else in my closed-door office. He resumes. "I will see you at Giorgio's at 7:00 tonight." Eric, who is usually all smiles, has a serious look on his face as he turns and opens my door. "See you tonight." He closes the door behind himself as he walks out.

I'm now standing alone in my office staring at a closed door. I can't move. I can't speak. I don't know what to do. Eric is already dead. He must be to know about The Agency and to know my name is Len. I walk to my chair and sit down. I think I'm in a state of shock when there's a knock on my closed door. I almost fall out of my chair as the sound brings me back to reality.

"Uh... come in."

"Hey, good morning. Everything okay?" Shay asks as she opens my door and peeks her head inside.

"Yeah. Yeah, everything is okay. Good... morning." I respond.

"I just heard some loud yelling from in here and wanted to make sure you were okay."

"Oh. Oh yeah, I'm fine. Had a... phone call... but yeah. I'm fine. Thanks."

Shay has a look on her face as if she doesn't believe me but she takes my word for it. "Okay. You want me to leave this open?" she asks.

"No. Close it."

"Sure. Don't forget that we have the conference call. Oh, and I sent you the memorandum that I drew up. You can electronically sign it and send it back."

"Yeah, I saw that you sent me something, but I didn't open it. I'll do that first thing."

"Thanks." Shay closes my door. Just as my door closes, my phone vibrates, and I'm startled again. I look at it and it's a text from Dorothy. "Good morning. Wishing you a good day. Stay focused. You're going to do well tomorrow night." I don't know how to or if I should respond. Based on what Eric just told me, everyone is lying to me including Dorothy. Yet, if I don't respond, she may think something is wrong and alert the team.

"Thanks Dorothy! I'm ready to work my assignment!" I text back.

I put the phone back down and stare into nowhere. I don't know what to do. I don't know how Eric expects me to work today after what he just told me. I can't focus on any-thing but getting out of this situation. Now I have one million more questions than the million I had when this all started. I have to wait until 7:00 for Eric to fill me in on what's going on. I feel like jumping up and running through the wall to get to him.

"OK Len think... think..."

I pick up my phone and text Eric. "Let's do lunch. Away from the office." I send the text and put my phone down to await his response.

I close my eyes and put my hands together. "God... I don't know if you can hear me but if there is any way I can get out of... please... help me..."

My phone vibrates. "Sure. Noon? Girogio's isn't open yet." Eric texts back.

"Early lunch. Make it 11:00. I don't care where we go." I quickly respond. If I had my way we would leave right now. Even waiting until 11:00 is going to be torture. There's no way I would've made it to 7:00 tonight.

"11:00 it is. I'll tell Reggie that I need to take an early lunch. Meet me at Spilled Milk on Columbia and 8th St."

Spilled Milk is a new breakfast bar in town. In my be-forelife, a few friends and I were considering investing in an establishment similar. Customers can come and have any breakfast ranging from Frosted Flakes cereal to hot oatmeal.

I arrive at 10:50 a.m. I had been suffering since Eric told me that he escaped from The Agency. I need to know how he got out and when I can make my exit. I'll do anything to be free of this existence. I checked my watch, my phone and my computer for the time over 300 times as I nervously awaited 11:00 a.m. When the clock hit 10:30, I left. I couldn't wait any longer. When I walked out, I didn't see Eric at his desk. I assumed he had already left. Now I'm seated in the breakfast bar and he hasn't arrived.

I fielded text messages from Randy and JaQuita. A nor-mal check-in from Randy and a useless text from JaQuita. JaQuita sent me a text to tell me that Angela hasn't men-tioned meeting me yet. I know we are very detailed in The Agency but you don't have to tell me that she hasn't men-tioned me. The entire thing may prove to be irrelevant any-way if what I'm hoping is true. I'm hoping that Eric can show me how to get out of The Agency forever.

I'm so anxious for Eric to arrive, I'm sweating. I check my watch again and I'm still early. To try to pass the time and not lose my mind from being anxious, I browse through the cereal selections offered here at Spilled Milk. The selection of breakfast cereals brings me back to my childhood. Every-thing from Sugar Smacks to Captain Crunch to Frosted Mini Wheats to Cheerios to Fruity Pebbles to CoCo Puffs. They have it all. I can't think of eating right now but I'm killing time looking through the selections. They offer every type of milk from low fat, to 2% to skim. I turn to my right and see Eric. He just walked in and is looking for me. I wave him over quickly and return to where I was seated. I chose a seat toward the side of the room because its more secluded.

"Hey Len." Eric says as he seems to survey the room before he sits down. Gone is the fun jovial Eric that I just met last week. Now he's as serious as one of the attorneys at Angela's firm.

"Let's start there! You know my beforelife name! How were you with The Agency and now you're out?"

"You want to get right to the point huh? You don't even want to know how I died or anything?" Eric replies.

"No! The first thing I want to know is how can I get out of The Agency! I'm willing to do anything!"

"Okay, let's get right into it then." Eric leans forward, crosses his arms and puts them on the table. I'm attentive and ready to do whatever he says I have to do. "The first thing you have to do if you want to get out of your assignment is abandon the mission. You have to agree to let go of your assignment and then go through the proper steps to leave The Agency. It's called a Journey World Renouncement. By renouncing your assignment, you're letting the world know that you are no longer interested in doing work for The Agency. Your journey is now taking a different direction than what The Agency told you. They told you if you don't work your assignment, then you will go to Hell. They told you that Hell was your only journey. Well that's not true. Your journey can change after death and I'm going to show you how to do it."

At this moment, I couldn't be any happier. The most dreaded thing that has ever happened to me is about to be lifted from me. I'm almost afraid to believe it. I want to cry, run and leap for joy. I want to hug everybody that I pass by in the street.

"So you said it's called a Journey... World..."

"Journey World Renouncement." Eric says. "I can get you all set up with it but the first thing you have to do is renounce your assignment. Quit your assignment! Never contact Angela. Once you agree to renounce your assignment, you'll meet with a Renouncement Committee to..."

My head is down because I'm taking notes of everything Eric is saying. Before he began his first sentence, I had my pen and paper. I dare not use my iPad for fear that The Agency may monitor my devices. I slowly lift my head to see why Eric stopped speaking. He was in the middle of a sentence and he stopped. As I look at his face, I can tell that he's looking at something behind me. He even smiles at whatever he is looking at. "What are you looking at?" As soon as I begin to turn around to see what Eric is looking at, I feel a huge hand slam down on my shoulder and grab me. "Hey!" I turn around to see that it's Josh grabbing me forcefully and literally picking me up out of my chair. My chair topples over, and I hear a few people in Spilled Milk gasp. Josh throws his huge arms around me and starts to drag me out of the cereal bar. I frantically look back at Eric who is calmly seated like nothing is happening. He smiles at me and calmly picks up the Spilled Milk menu sheet.

Despite my attempt to get away from Josh, he drags me out the front door. I'm so shocked that I can't even scream. Only the word "Help..." comes out of my mouth before Josh tries to put me into the SUV that I've become so familiar with. The same SUV I rode in for training since this ordeal began is back. Kevin emerges from the driver's side to help Josh get me in. Kevin punches me in the stomach which takes my wind away. As I bend over in pain, they shove me in the back seat next to a man I've never seen. Josh jumps in next to me and Kevin jumps into the driver seat. They slam the doors and Kevin drives away.

Josh is holding his huge arm across my chest which is keeping me from trying to escape. I'm in between him and another man that I don't know. The man that I don't know is looking about as confused as I feel. At the moment we turn the corner, Alexander turns around in the passenger seat.

"You care to explain what that was about?" he asks me in a very irritated tone.

"I think you're the one who needs to do some explaining! You've lied to me! All of you have been lying to me! How can I get out of The Agency? Huh! Tell me now!"

Alexander looks at Kevin and says something to him that I can't hear. Kevin immediately pulls the truck over.

"Let him out." Alexander says.

Josh opens the door and gets out which allows me to get out as well. Josh grabs me so I don't take off running. He is so big, there's no way I can get away.

"Let's walk." Alexander says.

The three of us, Alexander, Josh and I begin to walk down the street like we decided to get out of the office and enjoy the great weather. Much to the contrary however, there is chaos going on in my mind and I need answers.

"How can I get out of The Agency?" I ask.

"I told you before Brian, there is no out! If there was an out, we'd all be out!" Alexander states. "I'd be out! Josh would be out! We'd all be out!"

"Then why did my coworker come up to me and tell me that he was in The Agency and he got out? How did he know my name is Len? Why did he tell me that everything you told me is a lie?" I scream. At this point, I don't care who hears me. I don't care that we're in the middle of downtown and it's almost lunch time. There are people around and I don't care if I cause a scene. In this moment, I'm fighting for my life... what's left of it. I don't want to go to Hell and I'm willing to do whatever it takes to avoid going back. "How did Eric work for The Agency and now he doesn't?"

"Eric never worked for The Agency you idiot! Eric is a Ministering Angel! Didn't you see him glowing?" Alexander says loudly, matching my volume.

"Wh... what?" I'm shocked speechless again.

"He's a Ministering Angel! He was sitting there playing you like a fiddle! You aren't using what you were taught so you didn't see him glowing! The minute he realized that you don't know who he is, he began setting you up to get you off your assignment!"

I don't know what to say. I'm staring at Alexander the same way I did when I learned of my assignment. There is a moment of silence that feels so tense it can be cut with a knife. Alexander rubs his temples like he's stressed out and speaks to Josh. "I can take it from here. Tell Brandon that I'm going to need about five minutes."

"Sure. No problem." Josh responds. Josh turns to me and pats me on the shoulder with his heavy hand. "Good to see you again Brian. No hard feelings." Josh smiles and walks back to the SUV where Kevin and the other man have been waiting. I don't respond to Josh as I'm still in a somewhat state of shock.

"Brian. Dude. You can't do stuff like this! You are on an important assignment and I don't have time to fly in and rescue you! The only reason I caught you this time is we were driving by and I saw you walk into the restaurant. I then saw the angel walk in and we pulled over. If I hadn't been driving by at that exact moment, you'd still be in there talking to him and probably believing everything he was saying."

"I don't know what to believe." These are the only words I can come up with.

"I've never led you wrong. If there was a way to get out of this situation, I wouldn't be standing here talking to you. There is no way out. The best we can do is prolong it. I want to be here for one million years, but I need you to help me do that." Alexander says.

"But what about the Renouncement?" I ask.

"The what?"

"The Journey World Renouncement. It's where you can renounce and get back to..."

"Brian, he made that up! There's no such thing!" Alexander cuts me off. "Look, I don't have time to go back and forth about this right now. I can't run late. I gotta go. I'm going to send you a training module tonight that you have to watch. You should be able to detect a Ministering Angel! Get in your car and go back to work. Don't let this happen again!"

Alexander extends his hand to me to shake his hand. I take his hand and shake it.

"I'm... I'm sorry." I say.

"We'll talk about it some other time. I have to go. Watch the training module tonight."

"Okay."

Alexander turns to walk back to the SUV. I need a moment so I'm not going back to my car yet.

"Hey! Who's the guy in the back seat?" I ask.

Alexander doesn't turn back to me but responds loud enough that I can hear him. "Brandon. My new inductee. I'm his Chief Presenter."

I step back into the office in a daze. Now I'm afraid of running into Eric in the office. I didn't see him back at Spilled Milk. I'm sure he left after the commotion of Josh dragging me out. Walking back to my office, I notice a few co-workers standing by Eric's desk. I also notice a police officer standing there. I don't see Eric.

"Hey. What's going on?" I ask Shay as I approach the small crowd around Eric's area.

"Eric just got fired and they're cleaning out his desk." Shay says.

"What? Wait... what?"

"Yeah, I'm so surprised. He seemed like such a nice kid."

"He got... fired? When?" I ask.

"Just a little while ago. Apparently he's been stealing money from the company. They've been monitoring it for a while I guess. I don't really know the details. Ask Reggie. He knows more than me." Shay states.

"Where's Eric now?" I ask.

"They took him out. He was escorted out of the building by the cops. It was crazy! You missed it!"

When I walk into the door to my place, I almost want to turn my phone off. I'm so embarrassed that I allowed a Ministering Angel to trick me into believing him. I could've blown my entire assignment. If Alexander and the guys hadn't been driving by, I would've done anything Eric told me to do. I don't know how the others on the team are going to respond. They may become angry and lash out. Especially a person as loud as Carlos. I also recognize that I don't have the luxury of turning my phone off.

I didn't eat lunch and I'm still not hungry. As usual, dinner is prepared and waiting for me. I don't get it. Instead, I sit down and begin to weep. I can't get out.

My phone rings. It's Alexander.

"Hey."

"Hey Brian. Listen, I don't have a lot of time. I have to get back to work. Couple things. First, I'm going to text you a link. I need you to download the app that corresponds to the Angel training. The one you need is part four. Do that as soon as we hang up."

"Okay. Sure." I say.

"You're going to need to complete that tonight."

"Okay. I'll get it now."

"What happened today can never happen again. You jeopardized the entire mission and could've sent a lot of people back to Hell." Alexander says.

"I know. It won't happen again."

"How do you know that? Huh? How do you know that? You followed that Angel like a puppy following his owner! You're supposed to be the lead on an interactive assignment,

Brian! The lead! You got selected for this assignment because you were ruthless in your beforelife! The deals you cut in your marketing firm won that company millions of dollars and you were relentless! That's why you got this! Stop feeling sorry about yourself and this situation and get to work! You can be here for a million years if you focus! Come on man! You can do this! You're the strongest new inductee I've ever worked with! Get yourself together and let's get this thing done! I'm not trying to go back to that place because of you! I know you don't want to go back either!"

I've never had Alexander raise his voice at me. I feel like a child being scolded by an angry parent. Everything he's saying is correct. I am better than this and I don't want to go back to Hell anymore than he does.

"You're right! You're absolutely right! I promise you... nothing like this will ever happen again! I won't jeopardize my assignment!"

There is a moment of silence.

"I just sent you the text. Go download the app and learn how to detect Ministering Angels." Alexander hangs up without saying goodbye.

I see the text and click on the link and the training app immediately begins to download onto my phone. The Agency Angel Training Series. There are four parts to it. Alexander mentioned that I need to look at part four. I click on part four entitled Detecting Ministering Angels. Part Four takes a few seconds to download and a video begins. It's Dr. Reynolds from the training classes.

"Hello Agency Member. This is Dr. Reynolds, Instructor Priest from The Fall of Life and the Fall of Man course. Thank you for taking the time to learn all that you can about the angelic realm. This will undoubtedly help you with your assignment. Pay close attention."

"When it comes to angels, Ministering Angels in particular, they are on a mission to disrupt the assignments we are all on. That obviously works against our purpose as The Agency. There is good news though. The one advantage that we have in the afterlife to protect ourselves from these angels is their glow. They can't turn the glow off. As long as you can see their glow, you will know who they are. If you know who they are, you can work against them or avoid them totally. This training will help explain what the glow is and how to detect it. This training will also break down the methods the Ministering Angels may use to disrupt your assignment. So like I mentioned, pay close attention. This training can help you avoid Hell for a very long time."

Two words come across the screen. The Glow.

"If you remember The Fall of Life and the Fall of Man course, I spoke of the glow that Ministering Angels have around them. That glow is called glory. In defining glory, it's easiest to define in human terms so that you'll understand. In doing that though, I have to use the scriptures as those are the basis for all of this. With that, let's get into it."

Dr. Reynold's image fades away and words come across the screen.

"And the Lord said unto Moses, I will do this thing also that thou hast spoken: for thou hast found grace in my sight, and I know thee by name. And Moses said, I beseech thee, show me thy glory. And he said, I will make all my goodness pass before thee, and I will proclaim the name of the Lord before thee, and will be gracious to whom I will be gracious, and will show mercy on whom I will show mercy. And he said, Thou can't see my face for no man shall see me and live. And the Lord said 'Behold, there is a place by me and thou shalt stand upon a rock. And it shall come to pass, while my glory passes by, that I will put thee in a clift of the rock, and will cover thee with my hand while I pass by. And I will take away my hand and thou shall see my back parts, but my face shall not be seen." Exodus 33:17-23.

The words fade and Dr. Reynolds reappears. "If a person is celebrated for an accomplishment, you would give that person credit. If a person scored the most point of any player in a professional sport, that player would be enshrined in the Hall of Fame as a credit to an awesome accomplishment. If we cheer that player on, we are giving that person glory for an achievement. The better the achievement, the more glory that individual deserves."

"In the scripture that you just read, it describes a conversation between God and Moses. When God began to give instructions to Moses, Moses asked if he could see God's glory. God responded by saying no. No man can see the face of God and live. However, he said he would hide Moses in a cave of a huge rock. Once Moses was safely hidden in the rock, God placed his hand over Moses so when God passed by, Moses wouldn't see his face. Once God's goodness passed, God removed his hand and Moses say the back of God."

"Many people have wondered how Moses was able to author the first five books of the Bible when he wasn't there. How did he describe creation and Adam and Eve and the flood of Noah when he hadn't been born yet? The answer is that he saw the back of God. In other words, he saw what God had already done and he began to write down what he saw. The first thing he wrote was 'In the beginning, God created the heavens and the Earth. And the Earth was without form and void. And darkness was on the face of the deep. And the Spirit of God hovered over the waters and then God said, Let there be light! And there was light, and it was good.' That, my friends, is Genesis 1:1. Moses wrote the entire book of Genesis, based on what he saw of God's glory."

"By God showing Moses his goodness, he was showing Moses all the good things that God had done. For those things, God gets glory. The thing about God though is that he does so many good things and he is so consistent with the good that he does, that his glory shines all the time. His glory is so bright and so outstanding that it literally shines."

"God's glory is so bright that it would kill any man that even looks at it. No living man can see glory. You can see the good works but you can't see the shine of his glory."

"When God gives the instructions to Moses to build the tabernacle in the wilderness, one of the important details was to tell the priests to change clothes after being in the presence of God. That was because the glory from his presence was so strong that the shine got all over the clothing. If the priests wore that shine outside of the tabernacle, it would do damage to the people."

"This holds true for Ministering Angels. They spend so much time in heaven and with God, the glory of God is all over them. The good works that God has done exudes onto these angels."

I find this very interesting. It's somewhat amazing. I never went to church on a consistent basis, so I would never have known all this. I may have visited on Easter. I remember my family all going and getting dressed up for that. I remember going on Mother's Day but for the most part, Sundays growing up for me was sleeping in late, food and football.

Dr. Reynolds fades again and more words appear.

"And after six days Jesus took Peter, James and John his brother and brought them up onto a high mountain. And was transfigured before them and his face did shine as the sun, and his raiment was white as the light. And behold, there appeared unto them Moses and Elijah talking with him." Matthew 17:1-3.

"When Moses died, the scriptures say that God hid his corpse. No one was able to find the dead body of Moses. The reason God did that was he wanted to fulfill Moses' request. Now that Moses is dead, he can look upon the glory of God and not die. You can't die if you're already dead. Fast forward all these years and Moses arrives on the mountain. He now can see Jesus in all the glory, shining from good works. Moses does not die at this point because he is already dead. Moses was finally granted what he asked of God in Exodus 33."

"This light shines so brightly that it carries over to Ministering Angels and we need to be able to detect them when we see them. Nothing pleases a Ministering Angel more than a member of The Agency that doesn't see their glow."

I pause the video in the ap. I begin to think about my short time with Eric. He totally played me. He came into my office happy-go-lucky from Day 1. He was energetic, smiling, jovial and likeable. He then offered me tickets to the game, knowing that I would want to go. I let my guard down and trusted him and he got me. This won't happen again. Ever.

"In order to see the shine of an angel, you have to renew your mind. In other words, you have to think different about what you look at on a day to day basis. For example, when you see a bird flying, instead of looking at the wings that give the bird flight, look for the wind that helps the bird fly. It's almost like ignoring a person who is talking to you. If a person is talking to you and you ignore them, you may hear their voice but you aren't listening to what they're saying."

"In this case, you may see something but you need to really see something. Look past what your eyes are relaying to you and use your mind to see."

"I'm going to show you an exercise that I want you to try. The more you practice this simply exercise, the more it may help you. Find a quarter and tape it to any mirror in your home. Using simple scotch tape, take the quarter to the mirror. After you tape the quarter using clear Scotch tape, see if you can see the other side of the coin. If heads is facing you, try to see tails. I know it sound impossible but try. The more you focus, you more it becomes clear that you're using a reflection."

"Human beings are a reflection of God's glory. One of the greatest works that God ever did was creating you and I and all human beings. We are the expression of the glory of God. When God sees people giving him glory through praise or good deeds, it is a reflection of what he intended for man. Use the reflection to see the other side of the quarter. Remember... it's a reflection. It is a mirror image of what is supposed to be. Keep trying... you'll see it."

"Lastly, I want to give you some insight on how Ministering Angels try and disrupt our assignments. You were taught in training a Ministering Angel can never reveal to a before-life human that they are an angel. It is strictly against their protocol and they never will do it. That can work in our favor but I will explain that later. In terms of what they can do, they try to disrupt our assignments by distracting us to other things."

"First they will test to see if we recognize them or not. If we do, then they may acknowledge that they know we are Agency members. If we don't, they will divert you from your task to something else."

That's exactly what Eric did! Once he knew that I didn't know who he was, he used the one thing that he knew I would cherish the most... my freedom. He knows I am desperate to be released from this prison sentence. I want more than anything to be free of this curse. It was a simple trick and would've worked if it had not been for Alexander driving by.

"Depending on how closely related the Ministering Angel is to your target assignment, they may say things to the beforelife individual that will disrupt your assignment. For example, if your interactive assignment is to keep your next-door neighbor from attending church, a Ministering Angel will continually invite them to church. You live next-door to the person and the Ministering Angel may be their coworker. You speak to the person after work and on weekends. They speak to the person all day from Monday to Friday. All the work you put in to discourage the person from attending church, the Ministering Angel is unravelling. They are inviting them to church every opportunity they get."

Dr. Reynolds pauses before he says his next point. "If you're watching this production right now, it is because you have been selected for an interactive assignment. The reason you were selected for your particular assignment is because you were excellent in what you did in your beforelife. Your assignment was hand picked for you based on who you were. I say that to encourage you. Don't let angels scare you. Don't allow them to disrupt your assignment. You have all the resources and backing of The Agency, the most powerful organization in the world. You can do your assignment!"

I stop the recording and slam my fist down. I'm angry with myself for not recognizing Eric for who he was and what he was trying to do. I quickly stand up and rush into the bathroom. I reach into my pocket looking for a quarter or some change. I don't have any. I look over my bathroom counter to put something on the mirror to test Dr. Reynolds theory. I put my toothbrush against the mirror. Not quite the effect Dr. Reynolds was trying to describe. I place the palm of my hand on the mirror. I don't see the inside of my palm because it is against the mirror. How does this work?

I grab my keys and rush out of my condo. I take the elevator back down to the garage and start my car. I'm replaying all the events from today in my mind over and over. The more I watch it unfold like a movie, the angrier I get. I drive through downtown and head toward the other part of town.

My phone rings as I stop at a red light. I look at my phone and it's Alexander. I immediately answer. "Hey man."

"Hey it's Alexander. Did you download the app?" he asks.

"Yeah. I already watched it."

"Good. What you think about it?

"It was just what I needed." I say.

"Good. I'm glad!" Alexander sounds relieved. "I was hoping you took what happened today very serious."

"You have no idea!"

"Good! You sound confident! I think the next time you run into an angel, you'll know."

"I'm still trying to figure out how that whole thing works man. Like the quarter on the mirror thing. That makes no sense to me!" I say.

Alexander laughs. "You must not have finished watching the recording."

"Huh?"

"At the end of the video, he says something about the quarter on the mirror thing being a joke. You can't see the other side of a quarter if it is taped to a mirror. But what that exercise does is it makes you focus. If you try to do that, you will focus and focus and refocus. Your eyes will literally strain. Then when you try that on a human, you may see an angel. Just use the same focus."

I'm speechless again. I don't know what to say.

"Are you okay?? Are you driving? Sounds like you're driving."

"Yeah."

"Where are you going?"

"I'm mad and I had to get out and drive. I got somewhere I want to go."

"What? Where?"

"I just need to see something. I'll be okay."

"Brian, you just can't go off drivi..."

"I said I'll be okay. I trust you... now I need you to trust me."

There is a moment of silence. "It's not that I don't trust you but if you go back, I go back. Brian, I don't want to go back."

"You won't. I won't either. Not for one million years."

There is another moment of silence.

"Trust me." I say. "We're not going back."

"OK."

I hang up with Alexander just as I arrive at my destination. I park across the street, turn my car off and get out. There are a few people on the front steps of the New Hope Homeless Facility in Duncan Square. I look at each of the people as they talk to one another. I close my eyes and reopen them. I begin to look closer. I remove all other thoughts from my mind. I forget about what happened with Eric. I forget about the conversation that I just had with Alexander. I focus on the five or six people in front of the homeless shelter. I focus just as hard as I was staring at my hand on the mirror. I don't know if I've ever wanted anything as bad as I want to see this glow.

The door to the homeless shelter opens and a man steps out. He smiles at the others in front of the shelter. The difference between him and the five or six others is that there is a yellowish orange glow around his entire body. He sits down on the steps and joins the others in conversation.

I can't move. It's as if I'm frozen still. In the dark of night, the only lights on this street in downtown Duncan Square are the street lights, a few cars going by and this Ministering Angel pretending to be a homeless man.

I slowly take a step back and open my car door. I get in and continue to look toward the angel. I can't take my eyes off him. He is conversing with the others on the steps. He never saw me.

I remember the training. A Ministering Angel cannot harm me. A Ministering Angel can never reveal to beforelife humans who he is. I take a quick moment to remember what Hell is like and I clinch my fists. I open my car door and step out. I slam the door shut, loud enough that it is heard across the street. Two of the men on the front step look up from their conversation and see me walking toward them. They pay me no attention. The angel then looks up and our eyes meet.

"Excuse me gentlemen." I say as I approach.

Everyone looks up but no one says anything.

"I'm wondering if you guys can help me out. I'm looking for my nephew. His name is Gerald but he goes by Little G on the street. My sister, his mom, is worried half to death. They got into it and well, you know how kids are. He been gone two days now." I say.

"How does he look?" one of the men says.

"Wait, you ain't the cops are you?" another man asks me.

I laugh. "No, no, no. Not at all. I work for a marketing firm. I'm just trying to find my nephew. That's all." I say with a smile.

"Your nephew," The angel says to me, "how does he look?"

"Um, he's about 5'9. Skinny. His trademark is a baseball hat that he always wears backward. I think that boy wears it in the shower!" I laugh.

"You seem to be laughing a lot. You don't seem too worried about a young man whose been missing for 48 hours." the Ministering Angel says to me.

"I know how kids are. He's probably hanging out at one of his boys' houses. His mom is worried but I told her to calm down. The only reason I'm here is because I promised her I would check to see if he was at New Hope."

The Ministering Angel hasn't taken his eyes off me since I approached. His gaze is dead locked onto my face. He is looking deep into my eyes. I'm not backing down. I'm showing him no fear."

"What's your name... in case I see him." he says to me.

"Brian. You can tell him that his uncle Brian is looking for him." I say staring directly back at him.

"Okay, Brian. If I see a skinny teenager with a baseball hat on backward, I'll definitely keep him under my... wing. I'll make sure he does the right thing." he says with a defiant smile.

"Thanks. You do that."

I begin to back away. "You guys have a good evening." I say. They nod and go back to their conversation. I turn and walk back to my car. Once in my car, I take one final look at the angel. He's still looking at me... glowing. I start my car and take off.

Café Ekemaj is a great evening spot. They have great décor and good drinks. Its one of the most popular spots in town as there seems to be something going on every night. Poetry and jazz night. Book reading night. Paint and sip night and now speed dating night. The attire is professional. No jeans or sneakers. No athletic gear. It is definitely a professional environment. In my beforelife, my frat brothers and I would love a place like this. We could come after work for happy hour and cigars and laugh about the same things we laughed about last homecoming.

JaQuita sent me a text that she and Angela are on their way. I replied just as I was parking to go into Ekemaj. I now have a habit of checking for Ministering Angels before I get out of my car. The coast is clear.

"Good evening, welcome to Café Ekemaj." the host smiles as she welcomes me.

"Hey, um, I heard there is some kind of cool event here tonight. One of the fellas told me about it but then he got called to do an overnight shift at the hospital, so he can't even be here. I just came anyway." I respond.

"Oh don't worry. This is our second time doing this event and it was jam packed last time. There will be plenty of people to mix and mingle with. Here take this and sign up here. We'll be getting started shortly."

"OK thanks." I smile back at her as I sign my name and email address and take my number. I look around the already crowded room. By the bar, ironically the game is about to start. Clifton Burgess is playing here tonight. I laugh to myself about almost having tickets. I sit at the bar and the bartender approaches me.

"How's it going man? he asks.

"Man, you know how it is. Trying to make it happen." I respond.

"Yes sir! What can I get for you?"

"Um, let me get a Woodford on the rocks."

"You got it." he says.

I look up at the flat screen behind the bar to see that the game is about to tip off. I turn around and scan the café again. I don't see JaQuita or Angela yet. I check my phone as my drink is placed in front of me.

"Good evening, good evening, good evening everyone! Welcome to Café Ekemaj! My name is Donté and I will be your host for the evening. So tonight's event should be fun filled and maybe we'll have a match made in heaven!"

Heaven. I wish.

"Now I know everybody in here ain't participating in the speed dating game and that's cool. Some are here to participate. Some are here to watch the basketball game. Some are here to watch the speed dating game. Whatever you want to do is cool. Just have a good time! The speed dating game is gonna start in 10 minutes so for those that signed up, listen up for the whistle sound. That's how you know we're getting started."

I look around the café again and I still don't see JaQuita and Angela. I pick up my phone to see if I've missed any messages. No messages. I look back up at the game at the exact moment my phone vibrates.

"We're here. Parking."

Game time. I get up from my chair and walk to the restroom. I enter and see one other guy in there. We nod at each other. I pretend to be checking myself out in the mirror until he leaves. Once he leaves, I look at myself in the mirror. I take a long look into my eyes. I stare at myself and ask myself if I really can do what I'm about to do. I turn on the water and cup my hands under the faucet. I splash water on my face and grab a hand towel. I dry my face and look into the mirror again. Another guy comes into the bathroom and I finish drying my face. I look at myself one final time and take a deep breath. I exhale and turn to leave the bathroom.

Just in the three minutes that I was in the restroom, the café seems to have gotten more crowded. I immediately look around the room and try to spot JaQuita and Angela. I see them toward the front and I make my way toward them. As I'm walking through the crowd, I see Angela look my way. We make eye contact and she looks at me strangely before she smiles.

"Hey... Brian right?" she says smiling.

"Yeah... Angela! The super attorney!" I say.

Angela laughs. "Yeah, whatever. This is my friend JaQuita. J, this is Brian. He works for a company we're representing now."

"Nice to meet you." I say to JaQuita.

"Nice to meet you too." JaQuita says back to me with a smile.

"You're here for this speed dating thing?" Angela asks me.

"Yeah! I'm mad though. My boy Eric told me about it and asked me to meet him here but he ain't even here." I say. "I so don't like these things. I probably wouldn't have come if he hadn't told me about it."

Angela laughs. "Yeah, big head over here dragged me out the house."

"Whatever!" JaQuita says.

"I wouldn't think you would do speed dating." I say. "I would think some lucky guy has you already locked up and he hid the key!"

"No such thing." Angela says confidently. "No one owns a key to me nor locks me anywhere... ever."

I playfully raise both of my hands to my shoulders suggesting that I am backing off. "My bad, my bad. I get it." Angela smiles as I laugh it off.

A whistle blows.

"Oh, the game must be starting. Y'all ready to have a little fun."

"Let's do it!" JaQuita says.

"I guess." Angela responds.

I follow the ladies to where Donté is standing. "Okay, ladies and gents, this is how the game works. These tables over here are reserved for the game. Everyone take a seat. When I blow the whistle, you talk to the person at your table. You will only have 60 seconds until the whistle blows. Once you hear it, each person will stand and move to their right to the next table. As soon as everyone is seated, I will blow the whistle to start the next round. So, everybody sit."

"Should I get started with you since I kinda already know you? Is that fair?" I say to Angela as we approach the tables.

"There is no fair in love and justice." She says as she steps aside for me to pull out her chair for her.

"Indeed!" I make a sweeping gesture to pull out her chair for her. I then turn and pull out the chair for JaQuita. Both women sit down. I then sit at the table with Angela.

"Okay everybody! The final instruction is you will see an index card and a pencil in front of you. As you go through the rounds, jot down any person who you would like to interact with have a connection with. If the person you write down also writes you down, you may have a love match made in Café Ekemaj heaven!" Donté says.

"Wow. This is gonna be funny." I say to Angela.

"Think so?" she responds.

"We're about to find out."

"Here we go!" Donté blows the whistle. "You got 60 seconds to talk! Go!"

"Hi, my name is Brian." I extend my hand toward Angela for her to shake it. She laughs heartily and takes my hand.

"You're silly... Angela."

"So can I call you Ang?"

"No."

We're both smiling at one another.

"Okay, so let's cut to the chase. I already know what you do for a living. But answer this. If you could change one thing about yourself, what would it be?" I ask.

"You gonna ask a deep question and we only got 60 seconds?"

"You only got 29 seconds."

"OK... one thing about myself... um... dang, 29 seconds...

I think I have a hard time separating my business self from my personal self. That's why my girl J got me out tonight. She knows I need to..."

The whistle blows.

"Switch seats!" Donté screams out.

"I didn't get to finish my statement!" Angela says jokingly as she stands to move.

"Hold that thought!" I tell her. I move to my right and sit across from someone else.

For the next 30 minutes, I make small talk and funny banter with 25 other women. At one point I sat directly across the room from Angela. We made eye contact and smiled. She then did a gesture where she was pointed her finger into her open mouth as if she was gagging herself from talking to the boring man in front of her. I smiled and nodded to show my approval of her joke.

The last person that I sit with is JaQuita. As soon as the whistle blows, we sit down. This is the final round as she was next to me when the game started but we moved opposite one another. Now we are matched together.

"How am I doing?" I ask her.

"You're doing great! Angela is really hard on men so the fact that you made her smile is good. I think her having met you before is what is good for us."

"Okay good."

"After this is over, I'm gonna encourage her to sit for a while and talk to you." JaQuita says.

"Alright. I had 60 seconds to make a good impression. I

hope I did."

"You go a whole team working with you so you got an advantage. She trust me with her life so she'll tell me anything about you that she feels good or bad about. Once I tell you, you can use that info against her ya know?" JaQuita says.

"I know how the game is played. I'm ready."

The whistle blows.

"Game over folks!" Donté announces. "I hope everyone had a great time and please bring your index cards here. Please make sure your name is on it. We're going to take about five or 10 minutes to go through them and see if there are any matches. Just hang around and someone will come and let you know! You'll find out any potential person that found you interesting enough to maybe want to see you again! Stay tuned! Please stop by the bar, get a drink or order an appetizer! See ya in a few."

JaQuita and I stand up and Angela joins us. She was only 1 table over.

"Well, that was... interesting." Angela says.

"Yeah. You got that right! Confirms for me why I'm single." JaQuita says to Angela.

I laugh. "Wow, was it that bad? No index cards for you huh?" I direct my question toward JaQuita.

"Nothing caught my attention. None of these guys are my type."

"Sorry to hear that. How about you Angela? Got an index card to turn in?"

"Nope. But I do have a question to answer." Angela says.

"A question to answer?"

"You asked me if I could change one thing about myself and I didn't get to finish my answer."

I smile. "Oh yeah. You started off so well and then the whistle blew. I'm actually very curious as to your answer."

"So why don't y'all sit down and find out right now?" JaQuita says. I need to step out and make a phone call anyway. I got a client that must be suffering from anxiety because she needs me to call her every hour to let her know about her project. Has no respect for my personal time. So I'll be right back." JaQuita says.

"Okay girl, I'll be right here."

JaQuita takes her phone from her purse and walks toward the door to step outside. It would definitely be too loud in here to make a phone call so it was a great diversion for us to use that as her excuse to walk away from me.

"Well... let's have a seat. No whistle this time!" I say laughing. Once again, I hold the chair for Angela. We sit. "So, you were saying?"

"I've actually had some time to think about my answer. A few of those guys were so lame that I kinda zoned out while they were talking and I thought about your question."

"Wow... that's savage of you!" I say laughing.

Angela laughs. "Well I wasn't trying to be rude, don't get me wrong. Its just that everyone says the same thing in the 60 second window. 'Wow, you're pretty!' "What do you do?' 'Do you have children?' 'Where do you see yourself in 5 years?' You were the only person that asked me a thought provoking question. If I could change something about myself. That made me pause and think a little bit."

"I'm glad I could showcase my superior intellectual skills!" I say with a big smile that causes her to laugh.

"Oh goodness. Silly." she replies. "Here's my answer after giving it some thought. I hope this doesn't get too personal or heavy for you. I know we kinda just met."

"It's fine. I'm a big boy. Go ahead."

"I don't forgive and move on easily. I've endured a lot of hurt and I have a hard time letting go."

Wow. The woman I am supposed to cause immeasurable pain and hurt to just admitted to me that she's been through a lot of pain and has a hard time moving on. This is heartbreaking, but I must stay the course. I can't go back.

"I'm sorry you've been hurt. I appreciate your willingness to open and share that. I think to an extent we've all been there." I say with a more serious tone.

"I guess one day I'll be a lot better at it than I am now." she says.

"Unless you actively work on it, you won't. Something like that just doesn't go away. You have to work on it. Being hurt, forgiving, and moving on with no ill will toward the person that hurt you isn't easy."

"Very true. So that's my answer. So what about you Mr. Big Time Marketing Exec. One thing you would change if you could." she says.

"Your last name." I say immediately without even thinking.

Angela looks as stunned as I feel. I honestly didn't think

before I said that but it was a Hell of a pick up line, if I must say so myself.

"Well OK. Pretty straight forward aren't we?"

"I said that without thinking... but if I thought about it, I probably wouldn't change that answer. Of course, getting to know you a lot better." I say with a smile. That answer surprised myself.

"Nice fix." she says. "You must have ladies falling all over you." Angela asks without asking.

"No. I don't. I work too much to have anything serious going on. I just started with The Paradigm Group but with my last job in my..." I was about to say beforelife, "...I was very busy. I juggled multiple projects at once. I led a team of people who were all experts. So I never had time. I worked weekends. I worked some holidays. I would be on call 24 hours. I had a lot of responsibility and I took it very serious."

"You seem like the serious type." she says. "When do you sleep?"

"Sleep is for losers. No offense if you're the sleepy type." That makes her laugh.

"I think we have the sleep thing in common. I can't sleep in. Like on Saturdays, I wake up. I can't just lay there. I gotta get up and do something. But most times I'm up real late reading through documents and files. So I stay up late and I get up early."

"We do have that in common then." I say. "When I crash, I crash pretty hard. But that may be five or six straight."

Both of our phones vibrate at the same time. They are both on the table. We both look at them and then back at each other.

"I think its rude to check your phone while conversing with someone but since they both went off at the same time, we got 60 seconds like that dumb game." Angela says.

I laugh. "Okaaaaay go!"

Mine is a text from JaQuita. "I just sent Angela a text that I'm catching an Uber home. I rode with her so she has her car to get home. Good luck Brian!" I put my phone back down. Angela reads her phone and turns and looks toward the door. She stands up to see if she can see JaQuita outside.

"Is everything OK? I ask.

"Um yeah," Angela answers me while still looking outside, "my friend just left."

"Left? Why? She sick or something?"

"She said she wasn't feeling well so she headed home but," Angela sits back down, "she didn't want to disturb me. She said she would let me know when she gets home."

"I'm sorry to hear that she's not feeling well." I offer.

"Yeah. She had been complaining but she still wanted to get me out of the house."

"I'm glad she did. It's good to see you outside of the office environment."

Angela pauses before she responds. "You seem real flirty. I gotta tell you that..."

"I hope I didn't offend you." I say as she pauses.

"No, you didn't. But like I said, I dealt with a lot of pain so I'm not really open to seeing anyone right now." she says.

"Oh, I definitely respect that. Like I said, my schedule is probably way too hectic for anything serious. You saw what kind of work environment they got me in at TPG and I'm just getting started. I just thought tonight would be fun with some laughs. Good to see you outside of the office."

"Same here. I definitely didn't come in here to meet anybody." she says.

Why is Randy calling me so early on a Sunday morning? I answer my phone. "Hey Randy."

"I heard last night went well." Randy says.

"Yeah it did. Well I hope it did. We had a nice conversation but she told me that she's not really open to seeing anyone right now. We talked for a little while after that and then I walked her to her car."

"Don't worry about that. We got plenty of time to get her to change her mind. What are you doing now?"

"I'm lying in bed."

"Get up and get over here. She's gonna be here soon."

"Where? What are you talki..."

"Starbucks. I'm at work and I got a text that Angela is gonna come through here to get her usual. You're gonna bump into her and make some small talk."

"Okay on my way." I say as I jump out of bed.

"Put me on speaker phone while you get dressed." Randy says.

"Okay." I turn the speaker phone on and rush into my bathroom to brush my teeth. "It's on."

"This is how you're gonna play this. Angela is very independent. She doesn't need anyone and she certainly doesn't need a man. So when you see her, offer to pay for her drink. She's gonna get offended."

I laugh so hard that toothpaste flies out of my mouth and splatters against my mirror. "What? Why in the waw would I wanna woffen haw?"

"What?" Randy asks.

I realize that he can't understand me because I still have toothpaste in my mouth. I rinse my mouth and repeat myself. "Why in the world would I want to offend her?" I repeat.

"Because you can apologize and use that as a chance to ask her out by inviting her to pay. JaQuita thinks it'll work. If nothing else, it'll make you look like you're quick on your feet and you're funny."

"Nice. I'm about to jump in the shower."

"Good. Get here as quickly as you can." Randy says.

"Sounds like a plan."

"Oh, and don't put on any cologne or anything. I got some Light Blue for you."

"Light Blue? The cologne? Dolce & Gabbana?" I ask.

"Yeah that's it. The cologne. It's her favorite scent on a man. Spray on a little when you get here."

Wow. These folks have really thought of everything. Dating is so much easier when you have the inside scoop on a person.

I jump in the shower, throw on some clothes and head down to my car. I'm on my way to Starbucks in 10 minutes flat. My phone vibrates and I don't remotely consider looking at it. Texting while driving is what got me in this situation in the first place. I hadn't even thought of how careful I drive now. I just recognized that I have both hands on the wheel and am driving below the speed limit. Subconsciously, I've grown a fear of car accidents and my behavior has adjusted accordingly. I don't check my phone until I arrive at Starbucks. It's a text from Dorothy wishing me a successful day and to remain focused. Indeed I will.

I text Randy. "I'm here." I look around the parking lot as I wait for Randy's response. There are cars parked throughout. There's a Staples, a CVS, a nail salon and a Subway sandwich shop here. It's a busy strip mall and people are going to and fro on this rainy Saturday morning.

"Drive around to the back of the building." Randy texts back.

I oblige and as I turn toward the back, I see him by the back door to Starbucks. He quickly walks over to my car and I open my window.

"Hey."

"Hey! Squirt a little of this on." He hands me the bottle of cologne.

I actually like Dolce & Gabanna as well. It isn't my favorite, nor did I own it. But it does smell nice. I apply just enough where she will notice it and not be overwhelmed by it. After all, who puts on cologne on a Sunday morning?

"She should be here shortly. Come in the front door. I'll make you a drink and you can just sit and read the paper or something until she shows up."

"Sounds like a plan." I say.

Randy goes back inside. I drive around to the front. I make sure I don't see Angela walking up before I exit my car and enter the Starbucks.

"Welcome to Starbucks!" one of the workers says to me. "What can I get for you today?"

"White Chocolate Mocha." I say. I look around to see if I

see Angela coming in. I don't see her. I see Randy come back from a back door. He helps another customer who is in line behind me. I pay and take a seat in one of the lounge chairs on the right. There is a USA Today in front of me so I pick it up and pretend to read it. I take out my phone as well.

I send a text to Dorothy. "Stay focused today!" I smile as I hit send as I know she will probably smile to see me text her what she normally sends me.

I take a look through the paper and I hear the door of Starbucks open. I look up but it's another customer walking out and not Angela walking in. I look back at the paper and start to read an article about a growing tech company. I hear the door open and two women walk in. They are talking and laughing with one another. I take a moment to look at them and wonder if they have any idea of the afterlife vs the be-forelife. I wonder if they realize how precious the time is they have right now. I wonder if they're making the right choices to avoid the predicament that Randy and I are in. I wish I could trade places with them. I'd do it in a heartbeat.

The door opens again and Angela walks in. She doesn't see me because she is lowering her umbrella. The Starbucks employee calls my name to let me know that my drink is ready. Angela still doesn't notice me. As I stand and walk toward the counter, she looks my way, squints and smiles. "Hey!"

"Hey lady! Are you following me now?" I ask with a smile. I lean in for a more familiar hug and she obliges me. As I bring her close to me, I hold her one second longer than the normal hug so she can smell me... and I can tell that she does. She doesn't acknowledge it though.

"I think it's you following me!" she says smiling.

"Hey, it's a small town." I take a sip from my cup. "What brings you this way on a Sunday morning?" I ask her as I sip my mocha again.

"I needed a pick me up because somebody had me out all hours of the night talking. I'd be no good without my morning java."

I laugh. "Oh somebody huh?"

"Hey Angela!" Randy says. I turn around and see Randy smiling at Angela from behind the counter. "The usual?"

"Yes sir. You know what I like!" Angela responds.

"You come in here that often?"

"Well it's on my way to the office and like I said, my java wakes me up. I got problems." She says laughing. I normally get the same thing and that guy Randy is the manager here. He makes my stuff a special kind of way. Just like I like it."

"That's cool. Got your own coffee maker guy. So what are you doing for the rest of the day?"

"Trying to relax before a busy week starts again tomorrow. I'm going to hit the gym because they got a spin class I was supposed to start last week but I couldn't make it. I worked last Sunday and after we wrapped up I had to tell the guys, I don't do Sundays!"

"As much as I say I don't work on Sundays, I always find myself doing something work related on a Sunday." I laugh before I continue. "It kinda comes with the territory with me I guess. I like being the boss but that comes with a lot of responsibility."

"I understand." she says. Angela may understand my work ethic but she hasn't the slightest clue what the plan is for her life if I have a say about it. Angela tries to step around me to get to the register. "Excuse me for a moment."

"Oh no, let me get that for you." I reach for my wallet.

"No, it's fine. I can pay for my own coffee." she says.

"Don't even worry about it. I got it." I take my card out of my wallet to put it into the Starbucks card reader.

Angela grabs my hand to prevent me from paying. "Look, I don't need you paying for my stuff Brian." Angela has a serious look on her face and her voice is raised a little.

"Um, Okay. I was just trying to..."

"I make my own money. I can pay for my own stuff. I don't need any help paying for a cup of coffee." She sticks her card into the credit card chip reader.

"Wow. I apologize. I didn't mean any offense."

Angela doesn't respond.

Randy is standing behind the register looking like he is shell shocked. He breaks the silence. "I'll get your cup started." He turns away as if he's embarrassed by my exchange with Angela.

There is a moment of silence where neither Angela nor I speak.

"I'm... sorry."

"It's okay. I didn't mean to fly off the handle like that. Like I told you, I've been hurt. I learned through being hurt that one of my pet peeves is people doing things for me as if I can't do for myself. I apologize for snapping at you."

I smile. "Just bring that same fire to trial and win my

case!" I say enthusiastically.

That causes the rough exterior of Angela to start to peel away. I again see the light of her smile. "Oh so if we win the case, then we call this even?" she says.

"No, I got a better idea. Forget the case. How about this? As a means of me apologizing for my overt male chauvinistic behavior, I will appropriately apologize by going on a non-date with you and allowing you to pay."

"What?"

"Let's go to dinner. It won't be a date. Neither of us is in a place where we want to date. But we'll pick a restaurant, go have good food and drinks, laugh and chat, and then you pay."

Angela is looking at me like I'm crazy, but her smile hasn't left her face.

"Your cup is ready, Ms. Angela." Randy says as he places her cup on the counter.

"Oh thank you so much Randy!" Angela says as she looks past me, over my shoulder, to acknowledge Randy. She places her attention back to me. "Let me get this straight. You want to take me to dinner, to apologize to me for assuming you could just pay for my coffee... and to do that, you want me to pay to prove that you recognize the fact that I have the means to pay for my own stuff and am independent?"

"You got it!" I say proudly.

Angela looks at me as if she is taking a moment to consider my offer. "Okay fine! Deal!"

I laugh loudly as I if I didn't believe she would agree to those terms. I almost don't believe it.

"I'll email you the details of our non date." I say as she turns to leave.

"You do that."

At our group meeting today, I expect the other Agency members on the team to be upset with me over the fiasco with the Ministering Angel. I was prepared to get chewed out for being so gullible. Instead though, the meeting has started off with plans for my non date with Angela. Randy opened the meeting by telling everyone that the Starbucks exchange went well. Everyone is pleased to hear that. I'm learning from them to focus on the positive and never on the negative. That's absolutely the best way to live your afterlife until He returns.

"I'm glad you did well, my new friend! This is shaping up nicely!" Carlos says.

"Thanks." I respond. "I'm doing my best under the circumstances."

"And that's all you need to do. Your best. You do your part, we all do our part, and we will get this Assignment done. I trust that is everyone's interest." Everyone nods or comments in the affirmative to Randy's statement.

"Where's JaQuita?" Dale asks. She didn't know about today's meeting?

"She sent out a text that said she would be running late. You didn't get that text?" Dorothy speaks directly to Dale.

"Wait, let me check." Dale takes his phone out of his shirt pocket and checks to see if he received a text from JaQuita. "Ah damn, I had my volume turned all the way down and I missed the text. Thanks."

"Where are you two going to go?" Dorothy turns her direction toward me and asks.

"I saw in Angela's member profile that she likes Italian food. She likes a good Japanese Steak House too but I thought we should go to Dylianno's. That's the best Italian restaurant in town."

"Not bad, bro!" Carlos says loudly. "That place is expensive! I can't even afford to go there on my little Agency salary." Carlos laughs but no one finds humor in his joke, including me. Randy moves on as if Carlos never made the joke.

"Remember, Angela isn't going to be impressed with your wealth. She makes good money and doesn't need yours. What's going to get her to fall for you is you. It's your personality. Your look. Your height. All the things that The Agency has turned you into. We know what she will fall in love with and you are it. Even if you were flat broke, she would love you."

"Wow!" I say.

"Well maybe not flat broke." Christine chimes in. Her comment gets the laugh response that Carlos wanted. He laughs with everyone else though. "She's not into charity cases so let's not go overboard." Christine is clearly being jovial as she is smiling. No one would suggest anything opposite of what she is saying. "I want to add this though, I think she is excited to go out with you. Even though you guys have declared this a non date, she's still excited. She booked an appointment to get her hair done right before the non date." Christine smiles as she says non date. "She didn't tell me why she booked the appointment but it's not her normal day. This date is a special occasion of sorts."

I see through the glass walls of this study room in the library that JaQuita has arrived and is walking toward our room. She opens the door to our room.

"Hey everybody. Sorry I'm late." She closes the door as she enters and takes her seat.

"How are you dear?" Dorothy asks her.

"I'm fine Ms. Dorothy. How are you? JaQuita answers her.

"I'm about as okay as I can be I guess."

"Alright, I got some news everyone." JaQuita says. "Angela called me and we spoke about Brian. She's kinda excited about the dinner date."

"Non date." Carlos says with a smile.

"Yeah, non date." JaQuita continues.

"Really?" I say.

"Yes! She thinks you're super handsome." JaQuita says with a smile.

Briefly, I feel a slight ego boost only to remember that I have no idea how I look to her. To me, I look like me. To her, I look like what The Agency knows she likes.

"Of course." Randy says. "She say anything else?"

"She did remind me that it's not a date. She says she's not trying to get anything started but as you all know, getting her out of the house hasn't been the easiest. So for her to be going out without me or some of her other friends, that was the hard part. That's what she was mainly talking about. Getting over herself and getting out of the house. And that Brian is handsome."

"This is great. Thanks for that update." Randy says. "One good thing about The Agency is how thorough the operation is. No stone unturned right?"

"Yes. Absolutely. The teams work very hard to avoid that place." Dorothy says.

It still amazes me how people have settled into the mind-set of The Agency and working their assignments. I absolutely understand the mindset to avoid Hell. Who wouldn't get that part? The part that baffles me is how they speak as if The Agency is this great organization that is wonderfully keeping them. Maybe I'm the one that's wrong and should see things their way.

"Can I ask you guys an honest question?" I say. Everyone turns toward me and the room goes silent. Carlos and JaQuita were whispering about something. Dale was looking at his laptop. Now everyone is looking at me. Before anyone acknowledges that I can ask, I ask my question. "Do you guys feel that The Agency is a great organization because they are prolonging the inevitable?"

"Yes!" Dorothy answers quickly.

"If it wasn't for The Agency, we'd all be there right now. You do realize that right?" Christine states and asks at the same time.

"Nobody wants to be in this situation Brian." Dale says. Fact is, we are. We just are. No getting out of it. We are." He closes his laptop and continues. "When I sat in my graduation for my first assignment with The Agency, I listened to the speakers. I don't know about you guys but at my graduation, there was a guy that has been with The Agency for more than 10,000 years! 10,000 years!" Dale repeats for emphasis. "He just keeps going from assignment to assignment. So yeah, I love The Agency man. I want to be that guy real bad. If I have to be here, let me be on this side of the equation. Not the other."

He makes perfect sense.

"I think I understand your question and why you asked

it." Randy says. Don't mistake our enthusiasm to work this assignment with any type of happiness in being in this situation. Nothing could be further from the truth. I'm sure you learned in your training that you have to embrace your time. Love your time and work your assignment. Now..." Randy pause and seems to choose his next words wisely. "...you're the lead on this assignment. Up until now, I've been leading you. Technically you should be leading us. Yes, you're the newest person here an I'm sure still a little shell shocked to being here and what your assignment is, but you need to snap out of it. We weren't going to discuss this part because The Agency way of doing this is to focus and keep things going in the right direction but... you sat down with a Ministering Angel and almost compromised this entire mission. Man, you have no idea how detrimental that could've been to yourself and all of us."

"I know. I'm sorry."

"Don't be sorry bro." Carlos says. "Just focus and take the lead. You're our guy. You're like our hero, bro. You can do this. The reason you got this assignment bro is because The Agency knows you can handle cut throat deals. This is as cut throat as it gets!"

"Brian, when I got this assignment to assist you I cried my eyes out for two weeks. I secretly wanted you to delay your coming on. I knew once you joined the team, its game on. I'm going to probably be the matron of honor in your wedding. I'm gonna be there when your children are bor..." JaQuita becomes emotional immediately and starts to cry. Dorothy gets up from her seat and places her arms around JaQuita who has quickly started sobbing.

"Don't mistake what this is, man. This is hard. Real hard. The truth is though, there's a lake of fire that we're going to get tossed in that burns. I don't want to go visit that lake. So if that means I work an assignment... I work an assignment." Randy says very solemnly.

"That's right!" JaQuita says through her tears. "As much as this is terrible, I'd kill my own daddy to not go to Hell. You asked for honestly, well there's my answer. The last dream I had about Hell was terrible! It felt like my skin was being scalded by a pot of boiling oil! The people were screaming and my face was on fire! I remember falling down a hill with so many people and the hill was burning! No! I don't want to go back! Do you?"

"No!" I reply strongly.

There's a moment of silence in the room. Since I've met these people on the team, this is the first time they've opened up to me in a manner that shows their weakness and vulnerability. We are not stoic machines doing an assignment. Even in the afterlife, we are real people with real emotions. This isn't easy but no one wants the alternative. No one does.

"Did we answer your question?" Dale says as he opens up his laptop again.

"Yeah. Thanks. Actually, you just said something interesting. You said when you attended the graduation of your first assignment. You've had an assignment before?" I ask Dale.

"Yeah, this one with you and Angela is my second. My first assignment was interactive for a man who had plans to build a church. I was his financial advisor as well."

"What happened?" I ask.

"He was really a good guy. Had a good heart and loved people. I think had he actually done the church thing, he would've done a lot of great work in the community." Dale leans back in his chair. "He was set up real well by his family. When his father died, he received an inheritance that was pretty substantial. His family was in the construction business and his dad left him a lot of money. Well it turns out, The Agency knew that he had a serious problem with people liking him. One of the reasons he was so friendly and outgoing is because he needed people to like him. He wanted people to love him. Although his love for people was truly from the heart, it would hurt him if someone didn't like him. The Agency knew this about him and used me and my former team to bring him down so he wouldn't ever start the church."

"How did you do that?"

"When he got the inheritance, I started to advice him to invest in certain funds that I knew would fail. Some of the other members of our team were posing as friends of his. I told him to suggest our investment strategies to everyone he knows. I told him that his money would multiply exponentially outside of the stock market. I told him that the returns would be historic and he bought in. He told just about everyone he knew to try my fund. In 1 year, I was managing all of his friends and half of his family. Once our team got the word to pull, it all came crashing down. I came out as a scam artist that stole everyone's money. People had invested their life savings with us and the money was all gone. Most of the people in his family were older. They had saved all of their lives to be able to retire. One couple lost over 200,000 that they had in savings and were left with less than 5,000 in their bank account!"

I'm shocked and in awe as I listen to this story.

Dale continues. "Everyone turned to him and blamed him for suggesting me. He started to frantically call me and I wouldn't answer. He didn't know what to do because all of a sudden, everyone hated him. Then he learned that one of his friends from college shot and killed me."

"What!" I almost scream out.

"It was an Agency member on my team. He supposedly shot and killed me and then was shot and killed by police. Neither of those things happened obviously. The killer of me and the police officer were both on the assignment with me. Once he found out that I was dead and everyone wanted his head too, he put a gun in his mouth and pulled the trigger."

My mouth is wide open. I can't say a word though, I have nothing.

"His purpose was to start that church. His father's company was going to build it and then he would step into the role of pastor. The pressure of approval and being liked by everybody was his undoing. Once he killed himself, that assignment was over for me and I was reassigned to you and Angela."

"So... so the church was the point and it never got built?" I ask.

"No, I didn't say it didn't get built. I said it didn't get built by him. The fact that he didn't do God's purpose doesn't mean that God's purpose won't get done. It just didn't get done through him. The church is being built right now by someone else. I haven't really been monitoring that project because I'm focused on you right now. The Agency has a new team trying to unravel the plan of the church but last I heard, it's being built right now.

As soon as I walk into my condo, I sit down and take out my tablet. I call Randy and he answers immediately.

"Hey Champ. What's up?" he says.

"I remember in training that there's a database of every member of The Agency. All over the world. Right?"

"Yeah. Why?"

"Can we access that database?" I ask.

"Access it?"

"Yeah. Is there a way to see if there are other members of The Agency living in the same city or working for a particular job or whatever?"

"You know, I never thought about it. I don't know. But why?" Randy asks me.

"I want to do a search for members of The Agency that might work at Dylianno's. I think it would be a good idea to have some reinforcement while me and Angela are there."

I can feel Randy smiling through the phone. He can sense that I'm finally breaking out of my scared shell and ready to tackle this assignment head on. "I had never thought of that but man, that's not a bad idea. Let me make a few phone calls and see what I can drum up for you."

"Thanks." I say. "I'm going online now to make a reservation at Dylianno's right now."

"Sounds like a plan. I'll get back to you asap."

As we hang up, I receive a text message from Dorothy. "Stay focused. Counting on you. You can do it. Be encouraged." I call Dorothy. "Hello?"

"Hi, it's me, Brian."

"Hello dear, is everything okay?"

"Yes, everything is fine. How are you?"

"I'm fine as well." she says.

"Can I ask you something Ms. Dorothy?"

"Sure. Anything."

"How did you die?"

"I passed away simply of old age. I lived a full life. I was married and had three wonderful children. They gave me seven grandchildren and I even had two great grandchildren. My husband passed before I did and my family was at my side when I took my last breath. Only one of my children wasn't present. He was trying to get to the nursing home but I don't remember seeing him. The last thing I remember is one of my daughters holding my hand and crying. I felt like I was going to sleep. I then opened my eyes, expecting to see my family or my son who was trying to make it there. Instead, I see fire everywhere. That was the worst shock and scare I had ever experienced. Once I met my Chief Presenter, I begged for a way out. I cried for a very long time. There's no way out Brian. So now, I'm here to do a mission. I'm not going to fail. We're not going to fail."

"We're not going to fail. We're not going back."

My phone rings and its Randy.

"I have Randy calling me. Let me go. Thank you for sharing your story. I'll share mine one day."

"You're welcome. Talk to you later. Stay focused."

I take Randy's call. "Hey man."

"Hey. I found out that you can go to the training facility and have them check the database. They know where each operative in The Agency works. If someone works at the restaurant, we can find out."

"Okay great! Thanks!" I say enthusiastically. "I'll stop by the facility on my way to work tomorrow morning. See what I can find out."

I find it so ironic that I drive so carefully now due to a car accident that killed me when the reality is I can no longer die from a car accident. I carefully make my way downtown and take a detour to drive toward the training facility. I already sent a text to Reggie and Shay, letting them know that I would be late this morning. I haven't been to the training facility since the last day of my training. I wonder if it will be full of new inductees like it was on my first day walking in.

I decided to come early as to avoid the potential traffic and heavy influx of people in the building. I also have to get to work. The workers that monitor the database are rotating 24 hour shifts so I know they'll be here manning the computers. Randy says they can pull up any operative in any location in the world.

The parking lot isn't as full as I remember, but again, it's early. The new inductee class with their Chief Presenters and security won't be here for another hour. Without that crowd of folks, the parking lot will look empty.

I enter the building to more of the same. The lobby looks completely different without 1,000 people in it. The people in the lobby now are either cleaning crew, security or a few receptionist type workers. I step aside to avoid the lady using the vacuum cleaner and walk up to the desk.

"Good morning, how may we help you?" I'm asked by a woman seated at the front desk. She's looks like she is of African descent. As soon as she speaks, I can tell that she is as her accent is strong.

"Hi. I'm here to see one of the workers on the 15th floor."

"Do you have this worker's name? she asks.

"Patrick."

"And your name is?" she asks as she picks her phone up.

"My name is Brian. I came through training last semester."

"OK hold on Brian."

Of all the people I remember from my time here in training, Patrick is one that stood out. I remember seeing him sitting at his cubicle and him saying that he worked for the Department of Transportation in his beforelife. That led him to the job he currently works with The Agency. That was my first time hearing that and it intrigued me how The Agency singles people out based on their beforelife. I was equally shocked when I learned of my assignment. What in the world did I do so wrong in my beforelife that warranted me the destruction of my entire family for generations?

"Okay Brian, you can go right up." She says as she hands me a badge. "Make sure this is visible at all times so you don't get stopped by security."

"Thank you."

I walk to the familiar elevator and take it up to the 15th floor. For once, I'm the only person on the elevator. When the doors open, I know exactly where to go. I walk through the door leading to the Media Control Center. The room is fully staffed as if no one left. I walk right past everyone. Not a single person lifts their head to acknowledge me. Each person is busy staring at a screen, talking into a headset or typing. At least a combination of the 3.

I enter the second room and a person actually acknowledges me. I tell the gentleman that I'm just passing through and he lets me continue. He did look at my badge however to ensure that I work for The Agency. Otherwise, how could I get in the building?

As I pass through the next door, Patrick is the first person I see. He's sitting at his desk, typing something into his computer. He has his back to me so he doesn't see me until I am almost up on him. He sees me through the reflection of his computer monitor and turns around.

"Hey Brian, what's up. Got your message. What you need?"

We shake hands. "I just need a quick favor. How long would it take you to find out if any Agency members work for Dylianno's downtown?"

"The Italian restaurant? The fancy, smancy place?"

"Yeah. The one and only." I say.

"Hold on. Should just take a second." Patrick spins around in his chair and begins typing quickly. Before I can ask him the question that I really came here for, he pulls up an Agency member that works at the restaurant. "Boom. There ya go." Patrick scoots his chair back so I can see his computer screen. On the screen is a young White man, maybe in his mid 30s. "That's Neil. He's one of the chefs there."

"Wow! That was quick!" I say. "Can I get a phone number for Neil or an email or something?"

"Yeah, sure. Let me pull it up." Patrick says as he scoots his chair back to the normal position and starts typing again. "Why did you need to find out who works there?" he asks me without turning from the computer.

"Part of an interactive assignment. I'm taking my assignee there and I wanted to see if I could have a little reinforcement if necessary." I respond.

"Totally get that! Whatever makes your assignment easier to do... do it! Aaaaaaaaaaaand here's his number." Patrick spins around in his chair again so I can have full view of his screen. I see Neil's phone number. I take out my phone and type it in.

"Thanks man! I really appreciate this. I owe you a drink or something."

Patrick laughs. "Okay. Don't forget you said that."

"Listen, there's one more thing I wanna know if you could look something up for me. I don't even know if you can do this or not but hey, I came all the way down here before work so I might as well ask."

"What's up?"

I pause before I ask. "Is there a way you can look up the reason I'm in The Agency and not in heaven based on my beforelife?"

"Well that's easy. I don't have to look that up. You never accepted Jesus Christ as your Lord and personal Savior. Your Chief Presenter didn't tell you that?" Patrick says in a condescending tone. I can tell he meant no harm but I guess he didn't understand the question I need to ask. I need to rephrase.

"Maybe I asked the question wrong. Let me think...how do I want to ask this." I pause again. This time, I take more time in choosing my words and I do them wisely. "Okay, when I look at the particular assignment that I was given, what did I do in my beforelife to be placed on such a hideous and cut-throat assignment? I mean, I hate my assignment and the only reason I'm gonna go through with it is because I can't face going to Hell. That fate is far worse than my assignment." I say.

"Yeah, I should be able to tell you that. Hold on." He spins back to his computer and begins typing away furiously on his keyboard. "What's your last name?"

"My real last name or the one The Agency gave me."

"Your new one." He responds without turning from his computer.

"Lampkin. Brian Lampkin."

Patrick doesn't respond. He types both my new first and last name. "Just so you now, every single person in The Agency would rather work their assignment then go back. That's across the board, not just you."

"Yeah but every single person isn't the lead on an inter-active assignment sentencing their own family to Hell." I respond.

"Well that's true. Wow, that is rough. But like you said, not as rough as... well... you know."

"Yeah. I know."

No further words are exchanged about my assignment as Patrick continues his search. "Okay so I got a few hits on your past. So you were a marketing exec."

"Yeah. That's what I did... well, still do now I guess."

Patrick is reading through what looks like is a profile of me on his screen. "Looks like you were pretty ruthless on you way up the ladder of success. You remember a woman named Lillian Marie Taylor?" he asks.

"Um yeah. I used to work with her at my first firm." I answer. I wonder why Lillian's name would be in my profile. I haven't seen her in years. We never dated. Never were friends outside of work.

"There was a promotion that you both were up for in 2006. Do you remember something about setting up a fake email account and doing some things with that account that would ensure she would be overlooked by upper management for the promotion?"

I stand speechless. Patrick turns around to see if I'm going to respond. I can't. I don't believe he has looked up something as insignificant as an email conspiracy.

Patrick turns back to his screen and reads so I can hear what it says. "Well says here that you created a false email account, took legitimate transaction activities and doctored the numbers, and then sent them as reports from an email that was supposed to be yours. When the reports were received by management, they were clearly doctored and false. Since the accounts seemed as if they came from you, you were called in. You then showed your actual email with the correct reports and implicated Lillian as a person of interest. You made it seem like she was out to get you so she created the fake account. It made sense. She got called in and said she never did it but they didn't believe her. Not only did you get the promotion, but they fired her." Patrick turns back around in his chair to face me. "You remember that?"

I can't speak.

He turns back to the screen. "Okay, let's go a little deeper." He types for a few seconds and pulls up another document. "Do you know Allyson Humphrey and uh... Sharon Williams? Oh and... this one is hard to pronounce. Nzingha..."

"Thabiso." I say. I remember each of the three women he

just named and immediately know where this is going.

"Yes, that's her. So I guess you remember Nzingha." Patrick says and asks at the same time. So it looks like you were quite the ladies man. You dated Allyson, Sharon and Nzingha at the same time but were lying to all of them."

"I can't believe something like that is in my profile! I wasn't married, I was just dating! Why is this in there and used against me?"

"Says here that you didn't just date them at the same time. You got engaged to Allyson on New Year's Eve and engaged to Sharon on Valentine's Day, a few weeks later." Patrick turns around in his chair and looks at me as if he's waiting for an explanation. I have none. After a brief moment, he turns back around and continues reading. "You convinced Nzingha to abort a baby that you fathered with her. You told her that you would meet her at the clinic but didn't show up. Instead, you spent the day at the grand opening of the new mall with Sharon since your firm did the marketing and fashion extravaganza for the mall. You remember that?"

"That's enough man." I say as I feel dejected.

"There's a lot more." he says. "The Agency systems go way back. Way... back. I can pull up things you may have done in grammar school that may contribute to your given assignment. Did you ever cheat another kid out of his lunch money?" Patrick's attempt at humor falls flat as I don't respond. I simply pat him on the shoulder as if I'm thanking him for his service. I turn to walk away.

"Seriously... you wanna hear more? I can pull up more." he says as I walk out of the room.

The nap that I tried to take before my non-date is a waste of time. I'm either too anxious about seeing Angela or the fact that my phone continues to vibrate from texts from Dorothy. In either case, I can't sleep. I might as well get up. Dorothy has sent me 11 encouraging text messages and 4 more that tell me that I should stay focused. I don't know why she wasn't a motivational texter in her beforelife. I pick up my phone and call Carlos.

"Hey man! You ready bro?" he answers.

"Yeah. I'm good. I found out we got an inside person at the restaurant so I'm going to reach out to him in a few. Just to be on the safe side." I say.

"Good work! That's an excellent idea! Now you're thinking!" Carlos says.

"Is Angela home now?" I ask.

"No. I saw her leave out earlier. I think it was for her hair appointment to meet you tonight. She hasn't come back yet." Carlos responds.

"I wanted to check to see how punctual she is. I'm about to get in the shower and get dressed." I say.

"She's very punctual. She'll be on time, that's a guarantee. I'll shoot you a text when I see her leave home to go meet you."

"Thanks. I appreciate that."

"Hey man, we all in this together! You're the lead and I got your back!"

"Thanks!"

The next call I make is to the number that Patrick gave

me when I was in the training facility.

"Hello?"

"Hello, is this Neil?" I ask.

"Yes, this is Neil. Who is this?"

"Neil my name is Brian. Brian Lampkin. I'm a member of The Agency too." There is a moment of silence after I say that and I quickly deduce that I probably just scared the crap out of Neil. "Don't worry, this call isn't bad news or anything. You're good."

"Oh! My heart dropped! I thought this was the phone call that none of us want to get!"

"I'm so sorry man, I didn't mean to scare you. I guess I should have thought about that and introduced myself differently."

"Give me a second to catch my breath. Hold on."

I can hear sounds in the background as if Neil is already at the restaurant. He literally takes a full 60 seconds before he picks the call back up.

"I'm back. Who are you?"

"Brian Lampkin. I work for The Agency and I understand that you work at Dylianno's." I answer.

"Yeah. That's my afterlife job. Why?"

"I'm the interactive on a big assignment and I'm going to be bringing my principle target to dinner tonight. I was hoping you could participate in my date tonight by doing me a favor."

"Okay. What you need?" he asks.

"Do you know somebody that works for us that wouldn't mind going to dinner tonight? What I want you to do is sit me and my date next to that person. At some point during the dinner, that person will choke on their food. I'll jump up and save them."

"Wow, that's a good idea! I'm sure your target will be impressed!" Neil says.

"I hope so. She's not impressed by wealth so my money won't work. I can't ask anyone on my own team to help at the restaurant because my principle target knows all of them. I need someone that she doesn't know to start choking."

"Hold on." Neil places me on hold for 5 seconds before he speaks to me again. "I'm calling a guy on my team right now. Maybe he can come with one of the females on the team so both of them can be in on it."

"Set it up, Neil! I owe you big time! Thanks!"

"Don't thank me yet. Let's see what my teammates say."

"Tell them that I'll pay for their dinner. They can order whatever they want."

"Big spender!" Neil says.

I laugh. I always frequented the finer establishments in my beforelife. Dining at a restaurant like Dylianno's is something I would do anyway. I could also afford to not only pay my meal but my date and maybe a few friends. Of course, now that I'm in the afterlife, money isn't an issue for me the same way. I don't have to put a certain amount aside for retirement anymore. I wish I still had to.

"You're in luck, Brian! I got a man and a woman on my team looking forward to a free meal! So when you get to the restaurant, I'll make sure you're seated in the same vicinity as them. That way you can get to him to save his life before any other patron in the restaurant does."

"Great! Thanks so much!" I say.

"How do you look so I'll know you when you come in?"

"I have no idea how I look. Remember? I don't know how you see me, I only see how I used to see myself."

Neil laughs. "Oh yeah, duh! I forgot."

I laugh as well. "I'm going to wear a blue sports jacket with a light blue shirt."

"Text me as you're getting out of your car at the valet. I'll make sure that I'm at the hostess table and ready to take you to them."

Dylianno's is well known for both the exquisite cuisine and the elaborate décor. Its funny how a place like this will get rave reviews because of the fine elegance yet can't hold a candle next to the normal cafeteria of The Agency training center. Upon entering the establishment, the first thing you notice is the fish tank. Its gorgeous. It's also huge. The fish tank runs the entire length of the restaurant. There are exotic salt water fish that swim the entire length of the extremely long tank. As you're eating dinner, pretty starfish swim by which add to the ambiance.

I'm 5 or 6 minutes away from the restaurant when I take the call from Carlos. "Hey! What's her status?"

"She just left the house bro! She looks fantastic! She got her hair done real nice!"

"Good, that means at least she's seeing this for more than a non-date or whatever she called it. Okay thanks, Carlos. Let me call JaQuita real quick."

"Okay, keep me posted!" Carlos says as I hang up and tell my phone to call JaQuita.

"Hi Brian. She's on the way!" JaQuita answers on the first ring.

"Yeah, I just spoke to Carlos. He saw her leave. He says she looks really good. That's a good sign. She got dressed up for me."

"Don't read too much into that. We're professional women. We always look sharp when we go out. Never fails."

"Understood." I say. "Anything else I need to know? Any last minute stuff?"

"Yeah. I wanna give you one word of advice that I know

no one else on our team will. This is probably the most important thing you're going to hear so listen up."

Wow. Okay. "Um, Okay. What is it?"

"Remember Hell."

"What?" I say loudly and swerve my car into the adjacent lane by accident. The driver that I almost hit blows his horn at me. "Excuse me?" I say back to JaQuita.

"Don't get caught up in good conversation or how good she looks or even how good she smells. Remember, we are doing this for a reason. We work for The Agency. Never forget that. The minute you start to fall for her, we're all doomed. You got picked to lead this assignment for a reason. You can do this, Brian."

Wow, I don't know if I needed to hear that or not but I'm glad she said it. I've been looking forward to tonight as if I was going out with a real women that I met at a networking event. This is no ordinary date though. I am on assignment and I have to be careful how I handle things with Angela. "You're right. Thanks for the words of advice. I definitely remember all too well what I'm trying to avoid. That last dream that I had before I graduated from training was the worst! I don't want to go there 1 second earlier than I have to. Thanks, I'll be ready."

"Good, I'll check back in once I hear from her of how it all went." she says.

JaQuita and I hang up and I try to clear my head as I see Dylianno's in the distance. "Remember Hell." I think to myself. How can I forget?

As I pull my car into the semi circle driveway in front of Dylianno's, I text Neil that I'm here. I step out of my car and hand my key to the young valet. He smiles at me and takes my car. I button my jacket and look around before I walk in the front door. As soon as I walk through the second set of doors, I see three people at the host desk. A young woman smiles at me and speaks. "Hi, welcome to Dylianno's. Are you dining alone?"

I almost don't hear her as Neil and I make eye contact. He nods at me as if we're both employed by the CIA and are on a secret mission. "No, I'm meeting someone for dinner. I'm early, so I know she hasn't arrived yet."

"Do you want to wait here for her or do you want to be seated?" she asks me.

"I'll sit at the table if there's one available." I respond.

"I'll take him." Neil says as he grabs a menu.

The woman smiles. "You can follow him sir. Enjoy your dinner."

I smile back as I follow Neil to my seat.

"Right this way, sir." Neil says as he turns and walks past the first part of the large fish tank.

As I walk toward the actual dining tables, I survey the restaurant to look for a couple that may work for The Agency. There are several couples already seated. Neil directs me toward the left in which there is an open table and a couple sitting next to it. They both seem to be in their mid 30s. They are both looking at their menus as I approach.

"Here you go sir. Your server will be with you shortly." Neil says as he steps aside for me to sit.

"Thank you."

"Oh and you mentioned that there would be someone dining with you. What's the name so I can direct them to your table?" he says as he hands me a menu.

"Angela Hamilton." I respond.

"Very good, sir. Enjoy." I see Neil glance at the couple as he turns to walk away. I'm nervous to even look in their direction so I take out my phone to waste time until Angela arrives. I'm surprised that I don't have a text from Dorothy instructing me to stay focused. No one on the team has reached out but I assume they don't want to interrupt. They are probably on pins and needles. I'm not. I have been under tough situations before and pressure never gets to me. I cannot compare my fate to anything I've experienced in my beforelife but I can deal with playing my part. When I remember the advice of JaQuita, it makes it easier to focus.

A waiter walks toward the couple seated next to me and introduces himself. He begins to explain today's soup specials when I see Neil walking toward me and Angela behind him. She looks stunning. She has on a blue dress as if we color coordinated our outfits. Remember Hell. I stand up as Neil steps aside for her to approach me.

Angela smiles at me as she extends her hand toward me. "Hey."

"Hey lady, good to see you." I take Angela's hand and politely cover hers with both of mine. I playfully bow. She giggles and allows Neil to pull her chair for her. She thanks him and takes a seat. I sit as well. Neil walks away after he gives Angela her menu.

"I'm glad we decided to do this. No pressure. Just good

food and good conversation." I say.

"And a lot less noise." Angela responds. "Not a date though."

"No. Not a date. I'm just hungry. Speaking of which, what do you think you want to order?"

Angela picks up her menu. "Nothing in the world like a good steak." she says. "And listen, I'm sorry that I reiterated that this is not a date but like I told you before, I'm not in a head space to date right now. Just not on my radar and I want to make sure we're clear on that."

"Say no more. I totally get it and I'm fine with that. Perfectly fine. I'm here for the food and this is a great place. You seem like a cool person so I have no issue with what you said."

"Good." she smiles. "So yeah, I like a good steak. Butterfly cut if they do that here. I've never ordered it that way here before."

"I like a good steak too but I'm kinda in the mood for chicken tonight. They got a great chicken dish here." I say as I glance at the menu.

"Oh, the chicken marsala?" she says. "I like it too."

"No, something else. It's not that. And now I don't even see it on the menu. Maybe the menu changed. Don't tell me I can't get the chicken that I really I like." With impeccable timing, our waitress walks to our table.

"Good evening, my name is Sharon and it will be my pleasure to serve you. Is this your first time dining with us?"

"No it isn't." I answer. "As a matter of fact, I'm familiar... well I thought I was familiar with your menu but I don't see the chicken dish that I like. It has tomato on top with this sauce and..."

"Santa Fe chicken." Sharon says with a smile.

"Yes! That's it. You don't have that anymore?"

"We do. It's not featured on the menu anymore but we still have it."

"Oh. I was about to be a very unhappy camper!"

"Oh no, we want to keep you satisfied so we definitely have what you would like. Can I get you started with a glass of wine?"

I gesture for Angela to be served first."

"Merlot." Angela says.

"For you sir?"

"Chardonnay."

"Very good. Our soup for the day is a New England clam chowder that's very good, it's my favorite. You can think about that and I'll be right back with your wine selections."

"Thank you very much, Sharon." I say. Sharon smiles and walks away.

"You know, this is going to be an interesting experiment." I say to Angela.

"Experiment? What are you talking about?"

"Well, we're going to quickly find out how interesting we both are. I don't like to talk about work when I'm not at work and this isn't a date so I don't want to talk about date type stuff. So it'll be interesting to see what we can come up with to entertain ourselves outside of that."

Angela laughs. "What do you consider date type stuff?"

"Well if this was a date, I'd be trying to get to know you better, trying to see if we may be a good fit with one another, stuff like that. I mean, I still want to get to know you but with no motive."

"I understand. Makes sense. We can still talk about that stuff. No motives. I like that a lot better. Just organic."

"Exactly. No pressure. Just talk." I respond.

Sharon returns with our drinks as another waiter approaches the couple beside us with their dinner. Both the man and the woman at the table beside us have ordered steaks that have come out sizzling. Sharon steps aside for a moment so the waiter can easily place his folding tray down for the other couple. Once he does, Sharon places our glasses on our table. "Chardonnay for you sir and Merlot for the beautiful lady."

"Thank you." Angela says.

"Are we celebrating a special occasion? Anniversary?" Sharon asks.

Before Angela can respond in the negative, I come up with an answer that I think will make her smile. "We're celebrating a victory in court actually. Our firm won a major case so we're celebrating tonight." That does make Angela smile.

"Well then congratulations!" Sharon says. "I hope you guys can represent me if I ever get in trouble. I'll be back with your food shortly." Sharon smiles and turns away.

"I guess you can see into the future huh?" Angela says.

If she only knew. I smile and raise my glass to toast her. "To the future."

Angela picks up her glass to meet mine over the table. "To the futu..."

"Oh my God he's choking! He's choking!" The lady from the couple next to us screams and stands to her feet. She is frantically pointing at her husband actor who is choking. Everyone in the restaurant immediately looks in their direction. "Somebody help him, he's choking!" She runs around the table to him and starts to smack him on his back to try to help him in his choking state. In her haste she knocks her own plate of food onto the floor.

I jump up out of my seat, dropping my glass of wine onto the table. My wine spills but that seems to be insignificant to both Angela and I. I quickly rush to the man who deserves an Academy Award nomination for his choking display. He is bent over his plate of sizzling steak, holding his throat with both hands and coughing to try and get air. I grab him by his shoulders and force him to stand up. His chair falls backward and his actress wife steps aside. She puts both of her hands over her mouth as if she is petrified of losing her dear husband. I pat him hard on the back twice which doesn't help his situation. I wrap both of my arms around his body as if doing the Heimlich maneuver. I thrust twice before giving one large thrust. On the third thrust, as if rehearsed, the man spits a piece of his steak onto the table. Everyone in the restaurants seems to gasp at the same time. The man starts coughing to catch his breath as I let him go and slowly, the other restaurants attendees begin to clap for me. I pick the man's chair up and help him sit back down. "Are you alright Sir?" I ask him as I begin to take his pulse.

Between coughs he answers. "Yes... yes I think I will be okay. Thank you! Thank you so much!"

"Yes, thank you so much! You saved my husband's life!"

The woman says as she hugs me.

"You're both very welcome. Just do me a favor." I respond.

"Yes, anything!" The woman says.

"Cut your steak into smaller pieces!" I say with a smile.

The man smiles and shakes my hand. The woman gives me a hug again as I walk back to my seat with Angela.

"You're a very lucky woman!" The woman leans over and speaks to Angela. Angela laughs.

"Oh we're not... thank you. He's a regular Superman." Angela says kindly back to the woman. Her answer actually causes me to laugh. She looks at me and smiles as she sees me laughing. I guess Angela felt it would be easier to play along with the woman thinking that she and I are in a relationship than to tell her the truth of our non-date. Little does she know that this woman knows more about our relationship than she does.

Our waitress Sharon walks back out along with the couple's waiter. "Oh my God, I heard you saved that man's life!"

"He was choking on a piece of steak and I just dislodged it." I say. Sorry that I spilled the wine on the table.

"Oh no, that's fine. Let me get that cleaned up and I'll get you another glass. No worries." Sharon walks away. The couple's waiter is tending to them and all seems to be coming back to normal in Dylianno's.

"Well, well, well. Didn't know you were an expert at saving lives." Angela says.

"I just did the first thing that came to mind. I'm glad it

worked. The Heimlich doesn't always work but in his case, it did."

"I'm glad you jumped to it! Very impressive!"

"Oh, it's no big deal. I'm sure anyone in here would probably do the same. I just happened to be the closest to him so I acted the fastest." I hope that my downplaying of my actions is gaining points with Angela.

Sharon returns with a new glass of wine for me to replace the one that I spilled in saving the gentleman's life. "Here ya go and your food is coming right now."

"Aww thank you. Much appreciated." I say. Just as I say that, our food comes out. It looks delicious and at this point, I actually am hungry. "Wow, looks great." I say. "I love this place, food is outstanding."

"Yeah, after your heroics, I'm definitely ready to eat." Angela says.

"Heroics!" I say while laughing. "Whatever! So I guess you're gonna tell the team at work that I'm Superman huh?"

"Yup! I sure am!" Angela says as she takes a bite of her steak. I'm gonna let the whole firm know that you got a big "S" on your chest under that shirt!"

I start to eat my chicken. It's as delicious as I remember in my beforelife. As good as it is though, all I can think about is if Angela is impressed with my heroic display enough to begin to see me as more than an associate. I've never had to go through such lengths to impress a woman to like me. At the same time, I've never had such pressure or the stakes been as high as with Angela. It is imperative to me and my entire team that whatever we try works and we accomplish this assignment. I can't afford to fail.

I arrive at the team meeting early and enthusiastic. I'm the first person to arrive at our normal library location. I did such a good job on my non-date with Angela that I'm eager to fill the team in with the details. JaQuita probably already knows as I'm sure Angela filled her in right away. I'm happy to let everyone else know that things went well. First to arrive is Dale who opens the glass study room door exactly five minutes after I came in and sat down.

"I see you're here early. I thought I would be first today." Dale says as he shakes my hand.

"Nope, I wanted to be first. Had a nice time with Angela last night and I'm pretty sure I impressed her big time. I'm happy to share the details once everyone gets here." I respond.

"Now that's what I'm talking about and I'm happy to hear it! Good job my man!" Dale shakes my hand again before he sits down. "I can't wait to hear all about it." He pulls out his tablet and starts to work on Excel spread sheets while we wait.

"What are you working on?" I ask.

"I have to email Angela her monthly statement of her investment accounts."

"Oh. Okay."

Dorothy and Christine walk into the room together. I greet them in the same manner as I did Dale and both seem pleased that my time with Angela was well spent. Next to arrive is Randy who is soon followed by Carlos. JaQuita is the last to arrive at the meeting.

"Now that everyone is here," Randy says, "let's hear how everything went. Seems like it went very well and that's definitely good news!"

"Very proud of you Brian." Dorothy says with a smile.

"Thanks. Yes, the non-date went very well. We met up at Dylianno's and had a great dinner. The conversation was light but we never really had a dull moment, especially with the stunt that I pulled." I smile.

"Wait... what stunt?" Randy says.

I respond with a big smile on my face. "OK remember when I asked you if we could find out if anyone in The Agency worked at Dylianno's?"

"Yeah?" Randy looks concerned.

"Well I did like you said and went to the training facility. I found out that one of the busboys at Dylianno's works for The Agency. So I reached out to him and asked him to help me. He invited a couple from his team for his assignment to the restaurant that night and made sure that I was seated next to them. Then when me and Angela were sitting there, the guy from The Agency starts to choke on his food! It was epic! I mean, they did a fantastic acting job. The lady jumped up and screamed, her food fell on the floor, he's coughing and bent over, it was crazy. So I jump up and start to act like I'm doing the Heimlich maneuver and I save his life right there on the spot! The entire restaurant started to clap for me and Angela was really impressed! I figure... since my money doesn't really move her, maybe her seeing me save a life will."

"Great idea boss man! I love it!" Carlos says.

"Okay yeah, that was a good idea." Randy says. "You had me scared for a minute. You can't go off and start planning things without letting the team know. That can backfire. Glad it worked out though. Good job."

"Wait a minute. So you think that being a hero wins a woman's heart?" Christine asks2?

"I think that's a little chauvinistic." Dorothy says.

"A little? Its plenty chauvinistic! Women aren't damsels in distress Brian. We don't need you to whip out your ladder and save our little kitty cat from being stuck in a tree." Christine says. "You could've done without that display."

Now I'm confused. Both Carlos and Randy said it was a great idea. Neil thought it was a great idea too. The ladies however are thinking something different." I wasn't trying to be chauvinistic... I just thought..."

"Well you thought wrong." Christine says with an attitude.

"Wow... I'm sorry." I don't know what to say.

"Okay, hold on. No need to get upset about it." JaQuita directs her comment toward Christine before she addresses me. "We know you meant well and that's good that you're taking extra effort with our assignment. We all need to go over and above what we need to do to make sure we stay on Earth. At the same time, you gotta make sure that your effort is moving us in the right direction. No point in wasted effort or misusing your time. Let's agree that from now on, no surprises. Make sure the entire team knows what you're doing. We're on the same team for a reason. We're all a part of her life in different capacities to help you... us... complete our assignment. None of us wants to go back to Hell. So let's just do our part and make sure we all know what the others are doing."

JaQuita has come in as the voice of reason. It's quite clear that the men and women are on different sides of the issue with this but the women are probably right. Men have never understood women. It makes perfect sense that The Agency would assign women to get close to Angela on different levels. That way they can assist a man who may screw the assignment up. I will definitely take heed going forward.

"Yes, I totally agree." Dorothy says. "That's great advice."

My phone acts as my alarm clock as the ringer wakes me up. I see that Christine is calling and I immediately sit up in my bed and wake up. "Hello!"

"Hi Brian, it's Christine. I hope I didn't wake you." She says.

"No, no, it's okay. Good morning, is everything okay?" I ask as I adjust my eyes to the sunlight peeping through my bedroom curtain.

"Everything is fine. I just wanted to call you to apologize for yesterday." Christine says.

"Yesterday? What happened yesterday?"

"I snapped at you and I want to apologize. I'm sorry."

"Oh it's fine. I understand that my attempt was taken the wrong way. I never even thought about it the way you presented it. I certainly didn't mean anything by it."

"No, it's my fault. The thing is, I'm petrified Brian. I'm scared that somehow or someway, I'm going to be sent back to..." she pauses, "... I can't even say it. I mean, I know at some point I..." Christine starts to cry. I can hear the crack in her voice and her breathing pattern change. "I'm sorry."

"We're all in the same position. I hate the thought of going back as much as you or anyone else in The Agency. That's why I have to do a much better job of being a team player. I have to make sure that everybody on this team, me, you, Randy, Dorothy, all of us are around for another ten thousand years."

"Make that twenty thousand and I'll be a little more comfortable." I'm glad Christine offers to break the intense tension with a little joke. I don't know if the human mind can fathom what twenty thousand years into the future looks like. I don't know if my mind can even consider the misery of living on Earth for twenty thousand years knowing what awaits me. At the same time, I don't want to spend twenty thousand seconds in Hell so I'm going to do all that I can to avoid it.

"You got a deal!" I say enthusiastically.

"Angela has an appointment at Dale's office this afternoon." Christine says.

"Yeah, I saw that on the calendar. He's giving her the monthly report and then I think they're supposed to discuss some options."

"Right. Well I'm gonna bump into her on the way there and ask her how her evening was. She told me that she was going to an event when I was doing her hair and I said that there must be a man involved. She laughed but didn't talk about you. So I'm going to ask her how it went and see what she says."

"OK. Let me know." I respond.

"I will, and sorry again. Hey no hard feelings right?" Christine extends me a virtual handshake through the phone with another apology.

I gladly virtual shake. "No hard feelings teammate. It's all good."

I walk into our meeting location in the library and this time I'm the last to arrive. That surprises me since I'm 5 minutes early. "Hey team, sorry I'm early late." I smile. I look at Randy and notice that he doesn't.

"Hey Brian." Christine says. "You're not late, we just decided to meet an hour early and we didn't tell you. We just wanted to talk about the team and make some adjustments."

"Adjustments?" I slowly sit down. "What kind of adjustments?" My smile is gone and now I'm concerned.

"We feel that the team would be better run by... a lady. Nothing against Randy. He's done a fantastic job getting us to this point. But now we need a female touch so we voted and I'm now in charge of the group." Christine says.

I look at Randy who shrugs at me but clearly looks upset. "Um, Okay. Can we do that? Just change leadership? Do we have to clear it with the Chief Presenter or something?"

"Nah bro." Carlos says. "As long as we accomplish the mission, Boo Boo the Fool can be in charge. We just need to finish the assignment."

"The bottom line" JaQuita jumps into the conversation, "is we need to make sure that we don't go back to Hell. I personally don't think Jesus is in any kind of hurry to come back so if he takes another million and a half years before he comes, then I wanna be here for every day of it. For that to happen, we need to get Angela to fall in love with you and have these babies. No disrespect to Randy at all. Randy," she turns toward Randy, "you know how I feel about you. This has nothing to do with anyone's inability to get it done. It's just that we may have some insight as women that you fellas may not think of and if we take this operative in that direction, we may see faster results."

"It's fine. It's all about the assignment." Randy says. "I honestly have no problem with changing roles. As long as we get this done."

I don't know if I believe Randy. His words say one thing but his facial expression and posture say another. I do agree with everyone who has spoken that the most important thing right now is to not burn too early. Whatever we have to do to ensure that is fine with me.

"How do you feel about this change Brian?" Dorothy asks. All eyes turn to me.

"Um... well first of all, I really think I need to be in on these secret meetings. I mean, who had the bright idea to meet without me? You all remember that I'm the lead on this assignment right?" I pause and no one responds. "So from now on, no more meetings without me. Second, I don't have a problem with the change in direction. I guess my little act of heroism at the restaurant really struck a cord with you ladies. Fine, I can take that. Point duly noted. Lastly, let me say this. I don't care who the lead person is. Randy, Christine, or Mickey Mouse. I'm the one who has to deliver on this assignment and I'm going to do it."

I look at each person on this team before I say another word. Randy, Dorothy, Carlos, Christine, Dale and JaQuita. I recognize that each of them is as scared as I am but none of them are in my shoes.

"I actually got up early today and went for a jog before I came here. While I was running, I thought about the complexity of this assignment. The only way I'm going to be able to really get this done is to distance myself from any feelings I may develop for Angela or any of her kids. So, I'm working on me. I've decided that I will not love her, I will hate her."

I will not love our babies, I will work my best to make sure all of us on this team don't go to Hell early. If that means sending every single one of them instead of me early, so be it. I'm not going back a day sooner that we have to. If a million years is the time, then we're gonna be here. Angela and her kids will be gone by then and she won't matter. We will all be on another assignment. The point is, we will still be here. I guarantee all of you that.'"

I extend my hand toward the middle of the table. Carlos reaches first and places his hand over mine. Randy catches on and places his hand over Carlos'. One by one, each member of the team reaches in until all of our hands are touching over the table.

"One team, one goal, one assignment!" I say enthusiastically. Everyone repeats and agrees.

We have a meeting today at the office with Angela and her team. Today will be the first day I've seen her since our non-date. We've exchanged a few texts, joking about the dinner. The ladies were right. She never even mentioned me saving that gentleman's life. She spoke about the jokes that I shared more than anything else. I did mention that I was looking forward to seeing her again today. She responded with a smile emoticon.

My phone rings as I am preparing some notes for today's meeting. It's JaQuita. "Good morning JaQuita." I say as I answer.

"No morning is a good morning when it can be your last morning." she says.

"I guess I never thought about it that way... and I hope I never do." I respond. "What can I do for you?"

"You know that Angela is on her way to your office but I wanted to show you something. I talked to her this morning because we're supposed to be getting together for drinks later. Look what she just said to me. I'm gonna send you a screenshot of our conversation OK?"

"Yeah, sure. Let me see it." I hold my phone down and wait for the text message to come from JaQuita.

Angela

...ain't you married yet questions. I hate that with a passion. Really insensitive.

Jaquita

Wow, sorry bestie.

Angela

Yeah. Really hurtful. I think they mean well. I don't know what they mean. It just isn't the right thing to talk about to someone who is coming out of a bad break up. My heart was shattered and all you care about is when am I going to get married...

 iMessage

Angela

and have kids. And you supposed to be my family.

Jaquita

Sorry Sis

Angela

I'm sorry. I'm texting you to death! :-D Now you see why I need a drink!

Jaquita

I got an idea for ya! Why don't you bring a guy to your family event?

 iMessage

Angela

What? You gonna lend me your blow up doll?

JaQuita

LoL! Shut up stoopid! I'm serious though! Take a man. Your family will think you're in a relationship and leave you alone.

Angela

Where am I supposed to get a man from?

JaQuita

What about that guy Brian who you're working...

iMessage

JaQuita

... the case for? You said y'all had a nice dinner.

Angela

No! He would probably think I was crazy if I asked him to go with me to a graduation!!

JaQuita

He's good looking!!!! Ask him!

Angela

He is handsome! He might say hell no. What if he says no?

iMessage

JaQuita

> You told me he was a great guy and really handsome. Why would he say no? Ask him and then you can enjoy the graduation with your fam.

Angela

> You know what? You right! I got a meeting at his office today. I'm gonna ask him to go with me.

JaQuita

> Cool! Let me know what he says. I want receipts!!!!

Angela

> LOL!!!!

 iMessage

Wow! JaQuita has set me up nicely! This is perfect! "Oh wow, this is good! That was a nice setup you just did!" I say.

"Well I do what I can." she says. I can tell that she smiled when she said it.

"Did you share this with anyone else?" I ask.

"No. Just you right now."

"Okay do me a favor and reach out to Christine. Let her know that I want to do a conference call with everyone so we can talk about the best way for me to approach this. This could be major if I play it right."

"I agree." JaQuita says. "We have to be on the same page with what you say and what you do to meet her people. I've never met any of her family so this would be major for the team."

"Right. I don't want to come up with my old plan like I did at the restaurant and it backfire like last time. I want to make sure that whatever I say and do will help us get toward the goal. She has to fall for me... like head over heels."

"That's exactly right! Okay I'll get the message out to everyone about the call. What time do you want to do it?"

"Let's do it tonight before you meet Angela for drinks. That way you can probably say a few things to her while you're at the bar that may help the cause."

"Okay great. I'll set it up with my work conference line and text you the call in info."

"Sounds good! Thanks again! Talk to you later!"

I look up from my desk as there is a knock on my door that gets my attention. I was reading over the notes for this morning's meeting. "Come in, it's open."

"Good morning. You got a second before we meet?" Angela steps into my office.

"Sure, come in."

Angela steps in and closes the door behind herself. I stand up and gesture for her to have a seat in the chair in front of my office.

"What's going on?" I ask as we both sit.

"Well first of all, how are you?" she asks with a smile.

"Oh, I'm good. No complaints over here. How about you? Everything going well with you?

"Yeah, I'm good."

"Should I be worried that you wanted to have a meeting before the meeting?" I say with a smile.

"You need to always worry with me!" Angela winks at me and smiles. "No seriously, I have a favor to ask of you. If you say no, I completely understand."

"Alright, shoot." I lean back in my chair and wait for her to invite me to her family function.

"My family is getting together for my little cousin's graduation. I wanted to know if you would go with me... as my date... but we're not really dating of course. But..."

"But you want to rent a boyfriend." I'm smiling so Angela knows that there is no pressure in what she is asking of me. I can tell she's nervous.

"Yes... well no, not like that. See, why you make it sound so bad!"

I laugh. "Because it is bad! How are you going to get me on the team so you can fool your kin folk?" I laugh harder.

"Look, you don't understand the scrutiny that I go through with them. They are ruthless with the marriage talk and I'm sick of it. If you could go with me, at least they wouldn't be hounding me about getting a man."

"But what if that backfires and they start asking you all kinds of questions about me?" I ask.

"I thought about that and I honestly think I'd prefer that to what they usually ask me. I'm sure my aunts are going to whisper about you and ask me some questions. I'll gladly take that compared to the text messages, voice mails and inboxes that I'll get from my family."

"Is it really that bad?"

"Yes. Since I just came out of a relationship with a bad breakup, I really don't want to go through that again. First it's, what happened to Jeff? Oh I loved him! Can't you get Jeff back? He was such a nice boy! Then it's, you should meet my next door neighbor's son! H got a good job and works at the bank! "

I change my tone to become more serious. "I get it. Well what do you need me to do? Just basically play wingman and smile a lot?"

"Just be my date. I know it's corny but I'll owe you big time Brian. Serious. I really appreciate it."

"No problem. I'm happy to help. Hey, maybe I'll have fun meeting your family."

"Well we're having a BBQ at my mother's house after the graduation ceremony. So it's funny you should say have fun because it actually is a lot of fun. Some of my uncles play cards. There's always a ton of food so it's a good time."

"Okay see now you're talking! I love family gatherings with food. Count me in!" I say.

"You're the best, Brian! Thanks!"

"Don't thank me yet. You haven't seen my terms and invoice."

"Oh really? Is that what we're doing?" she says with a big smile.

"Hey... business is business." I respond with a smile of my own.

Angela stands up. "Send your invoice to my people. I'll see that someone takes care of it asap."

"Uh huh."

"See ya in the meeting in a few minutes." Angela leaves my office.

"Good evening everyone, I think we're all on the call. Let's get started." Christine says. "We definitely want to discuss this new development in our assignment and see what the best way to go about it is. By now, we've all had a chance to see the text conversation between JaQuita and Angela and I believe Brian was invited by Angela. Is that correct Brian?"

"Yes. She came into my office today before our meeting and invited me to the graduation. Just like JaQuita said she would. She explained her family and the entire situation. I told her I would go and she was happy to hear that."

"That's great bro!" Carlos says. "That's really great!"

"This is Randy. So what is the game plan? What should Brian say versus not say at this event?"

I think Randy still feels bad about being removed from his position with the team. Normally he would make a suggestion or just state what the plan of action is. Now he's asking and I don't think he likes it.

"We definitely want to play this smart. Brian you can't come off as aggressive at all. At the end of the day, you have to look at this like you're doing her a favor." Christine responds. "The reason this is good is because Angela will probab..."

"Yeah well we know that." Randy interrupts. "We know he can't come off as pushy but what's the game plan?"

"Um excuse me, I was talking."

"I understand that but we need to know what the game plan is. What's the course of action. You're in charge right?"

I can clearly hear the attitude in Randy's voice now. He's bitter about being removed and has left no question about his feelings.

"Excuse me! Do you have a problem!" Christine responds back loud and harsh.

"Okay wait a minute..." Dorothy tries to gain some type of order on the conference call but it doesn't work.

Everyone is disheveled by Randy's response. People start to talk at the same time. On a conference call, that sounds like mayhem. I try to regain the order by making my voice louder than anyone else. "Hey! Hey! Hey! Stop! Everybody shut up!" That works.

"Thank you Bri..." Christine says.

"I said shut up! I'm talking now!" That works too. "None of you have to deal with what I'm going through Okay? None of you! I'm the one who has to do this to my children! I'm the one who has to watch my son and daughter grow up knowing I'm sending them to that place! When any of you have to sleep at night after having to deal with that, then you can argue about who is in charge! Until then, shut up! I hate Angela! I hate any offspring she brings into this world! I hate this assignment and I really don't like any of you, but we gotta work together or we all go back! So stop being stupid and let's do this!" My words are louder than my volume. There is a moment of dead silence on the phone. No one has thought of the emotional turmoil that I'm going through. I'm dead set on accomplishing this mission because I'm not trying to go back. I hope to have thousands more assignments before this is all over. I can't overly focus on this or any other assignment. Just perform it and move on.

"Everybody, Brian is right." Dale speaks up. "We can't waste time fighting amongst ourselves. If we do that, we go back to Hell and our Chief Presenters may go back too. That messes up a lot of stuff. So let's refocus and remember we're all on the same team."

"Okay." Christine sounds defeated.

"Christine, I don't think it was a bad idea for you to let us know the woman's perspective. Randy, there was nothing wrong with the way you were leading. With all that being said, I think we need to get this thing in order and get it right. So here's the fact... I never had a problem dating women in my beforelife, I won't have a problem now. So from here on out, this is how it goes. I'm in charge. I have the most to lose. I am open to all suggestions and criticisms from anyone. We can vote, we can agree to disagree. Whatever, but we are one team! One assignment! That's how we're going to be successful and that's how we're moving forward from this point!" I say confidently.

After a brief silence, "Sounds good to me." Dorothy chimes in in a motherly kind of way.

"That makes sense bro." Carlos comments. "I'm in."

"All I care about is not losing! We cannot lose!" JaQuita says. "We cannot go back! Whatever that means, I'm okay with that plan."

"I'm all for the team. I want us to stick around. Unlike Brian, I actually like you all." Randy laughs at his own suggestion that he likes everyone which breaks a little of the tension that he created. "I apologize to each of you for my rude behavior. We have to remember what's at stake here. I know that I can speak for all of us in saying that we don't want to go to Hell anytime soon. So this plan works for me. Christine I know you had some great things to offer that will help Brian get to Angela's heart. Please let us know that so we can get this assignment done and on to the next one."

"I'm sorry too guys. I know I came off very rude over the last few days." Christine says. "Honestly, I was very rude in my beforelife. Many of my closest friends would tell me that and I brushed them off. Even after all that has happened with me dying and being selected for The Agency, I'm still who I am. I can come off very abrasive and harsh but the bottom line like Brian said is to be here through this assignment. This assignment is hard but if we focus, this is only one of many. Let's get this done, however long it takes and move on to the next hundred. Randy, I'm sorry."

"Apology not necessary. We're fine." Randy says.

"Well now that we're all back on track," Dale says, "what is the plan for this graduation."

"How about this... I show up and do me. I won't try to overly impress Angela. I won't try to hit a home run on my first swing of the bat. I won't try to win her entire family over. She asked me to go as a date so she won't get the harassing questions. Why don't I do just that. I'll do what she asked without the made-up heroics. Let's see if Len... I mean Brian, can still work magic by just being me."

There is another moment of silence where it seems everyone is considering what I am saying. I plan to just be me.

"I think that is the most logical approach." Dale says.

"That makes one hundred percent total sense man! Just be yourself! I mean heck, if I was a girl, I'd go for ya!" Carlos says as he has a hardy laugh at his own corny joke. A few folks on the call laugh as well.

"Okay, in terms of moving forward with this graduation event, I do have an idea." Randy brings the conversation back to the point of our discussion. "I think one of us or maybe even two of us should be in your ear during the event. Almost like you were wearing a wire or something. We can communicate via text message. Just to monitor what's happening throughout the course of the event."

"That's a good idea." Dorothy says.

"Yes but you definitely don't want to keep checking your phone ever five minutes." Christine says. "Most women would see that as very rude. Especially when she's introducing you to her family."

"I agree." JaQuita agrees.

"So we keep it light. Maybe once an hour, just to check in. Just make sure everything is going smooth." Randy offers.

"Sounds like a good plan." I say. "Do you and Christine want to be the two people I communicate with?"

"Works for me." Randy says.

"Yeah, I'm up for that." Christine says.

"Great! I'm going to totally be myself and keep the team abreast of the entire day as much as I can without being obvious on my phone. That's the plan. Now let's go make it happen!"

I arrive at Angela's house as planned. I am on time and ready. I finally see both her and Carlos' homes. Both are nice homes with beautiful landscaping. I see Angela's car and I park right behind her car in the driveway. I text her to let her know that I have arrived. If almost on cue, Carlos' front door opens and he steps out with a bag of golf clubs over his shoulder. He turns and locks his door. As he walks toward his car in his driveway, Angela comes outside. She looks beautiful. She's wearing a powerful all white pants suit with a yellow scarf around her neck. Her hair is done differently than when I saw her in the meeting. Christine did a good job.

"Hi Carlos! Going to play Tiger Woods today!" Angela calls out to Carlos as he is getting in his car. He turns and smiles.

"Hey Neighbor! Yeah! I'm gonna go win the PGA Tour!" He laughs as he closes his car door and starts his engine.

I get out of my car to open my passenger door for Angela. I smile as she approaches me.

"That's Carlos, my neighbor. He is crazy but loveable. He looks out for me." she says as she waves to Carlos who is now driving in reverse down his driveway.

She has no idea how Carlos is actually looking out for her.

"You look nice. I love that suit." I say as I open her door.

"Thank you. You don't look half bad yourself."

I smile as I close her door. I walk around to get into the driver's seat. I take one last glance at Angela's home, then at Carlos' home before I get in.

"You smell great! Godmom is gonna love you!" Angela says.

"Oh yeah? Is she seeing anybody because I may have tickets to a jazz concert next weekend!"

"Shut up!" Angela says laughing.

I begin to drive toward her godmother's house. That's where the family is meeting before they drive together to the arena for the graduation. Angela actually emailed me a flowchart that lists all of her family members and who I can expect to meet today. She also sent a thorough explanation as to my role in her life. This woman is on point. It will be a difficult task to get her to fall for me and then to get her to follow me straight to Hell.

"Listen, I just want to thank you again for doing this. I normally would never do anything like this but I just want to go, celebrate my cousin and have a good day." Angela says.

"It's fine. I'm actually glad you asked me to do this. I would have probably sat on the couch all day today if you hadn't asked me to do this. Maybe gone out to go to the cleaners but other than that, I would have been bored at home. So far, you been out with me at the dating game thing, a great dinner besides a man next to us almost dying, and now this. So thank you for giving me more of a life outside of work."

Angela laughs. "Oh you're more than welcome. And you silly about that man dying. I've enjoyed spending time with you and I was so dreading this that it was almost making me sick. Like I felt like I wanted to throw up. I was talking to one of my girls about it and I was trying to get her to cosign with me to not go to the graduation at all. I couldn't do that to my cousin... he's a great kid. So I thought about inviting you and she said it was a good idea. You remember my girl JaQuita? She was at that dating thing with me."

"Oh yeah, I remember her." I say.

"She calmed my nerves about asking you. She said you seemed nice enough that I could ask."

"And I hope handsome enough." I look at Angela for the first time since I've been driving.

She turns away to look outside the window to attempt to hide her smile. This is one of those cute, awkward moments that can make or break the ice breaker minutes. She turns back to answer my non-question. "Yes, you are quite handsome. Just who my family would want to see me with. You smell good too."

"I took a shower for this special occasion." That makes Angela laugh and I laugh with her. "OK so you said your godmother lives in Springville Gardens? That's Exit 29 right?"

"Yeah, two more exits. You know where Springville Gardens is?" she asks.

"Well I know the vicinity but once we get off, you're going to have to tell me how to get to her house."

"OK no problem. That's where I grew up." Angela says. She looks back out the window.

"Oh yeah? You grew up near your godmother?" I ask.

"I grew up with my godmother. My Godmother has had legal custody of me since I was eleven years old. My mom was a single mother and she died in a car accident."

When Angela says her mother died in a car accident, I almost lose control of my car. I died in a car accident and now she's telling me that her mother died in a car accident. This is crazy.

"Oh wow, I'm sorry to hear that." I offer.

"Thank you but it's fine. I've learned to cope and deal with it. My godmother has been great. She came in and took over and became a real parent. She never let me call her mom because she never wanted me to forget my mother. She stepped in from day one and has been everything to..." I hear the crack in Angela's voice as she describes her godmother. She has becomes emotional as she tells me of this woman who is near and dear to her.

If JaQuita knew that Angela's godmother was so special to her, she certainly didn't tell me. I didn't know that Angela's parents weren't here. I would think that would be an important detail that my entire team should know.

"I'm sorry... I can't be crying like this and mess up my makeup." Angela laughs which breaks the emotional tension.

"Nothing wrong with letting out a little emotion. You just better get it together quick. We're gonna be there in a few minutes." I slow down to get off the exit 29 ramp. "Let me pull over to get gas. That will give you a few moments." I say.

"I'm okay." Angela says. Her voice is coming back to normal.

"I need to get gas anyway and I want to get some mints so my breath is fresh." I say with a smile. "Can't meet the family with halitosis!" I actually want to check my phone. I felt it vibrate twice already and I know it's Randy and Christine checking in.

Just off the exit there is a gas station to the right. I stop briefly at the light and turn right. I pull into the gas station and park at a pump. I turn my car engine off and turn to Angela. "Do you need anything from inside?" I ask.

"No, I'm fine." she replies.

I get out of the car and pay for the gas at the pump. As I stand at the back of the car, I notice Angela using her phone. I take my phone out of my pocket and see that I have a text from Randy. I quickly respond and place my phone back into my pocket.

JaQuita

So how is it going so far?
Carlos says he saw you
at Angela's house.
Everything going well?

Randy

Hey! Just letting you know
that we're both here and
ready to guide you if you
need anything. Are you
doing okay so far?

Brian

Hey Team! I'm good! I'm
stopped to get gas and to
check in. Why didn't
someone tell me that
Angela's mother is dead
and she was raised by
her godmother? Did you
guys know that?

📷 　 iMessage 　　　　 🎤

I finish topping my car off and I return the nozzle to the pump. I walk inside the gas station convenience store to purchase mints. As soon as I walk into the store, I take my phone out of my pocket as I felt it vibrate.

❮ **Messages**　**JaQuita, Randy**　Details

Brian

> Hey Team! I'm good! I'm stopped to get gas and to check in. Why didn't someone tell me that Angela's mother is dead and she was raised by her godmother? Did you guys know that?

JaQuita

> What??? I didn't know that! That's not in her file!

Randy

> I didn't know that either. I don't know anything about Angela's parents at all. I had no idea!

 iMessage

I purchase the mints and walk to my car. Angela puts her phone away as I start my car. "Okay, let's roll!" I say.

"Make a right out of the station and you're going to drive through four stoplights." Angela instructs me.

"So I looked through the family chart. I think I can remember all the names." I say.

"Oh yeah, so there's three people you need to remember. Everyone else it will be like you're meeting for the first time. Just keep in mind who the three are and you will have done well today, Sir."

"Oh OK well that's not bad at all. Who are the main three?" I ask.

"First, my godmother. Her name is Bernice. Second is her sister, Aunt Dia. Her full name is Diane but we all call her Dia. She's the nosey one. Aunt Dia is probably going to be in your face all day trying to figure out who you are and what your intentions are with her beloved niece, Angie."

I laugh after Angela laughs. I try to imagine what Aunt Dia looks like. I think everyone has someone in their family who can fit this personality trait.

"The third person is my Uncle Trevor. At some point he'll pull you aside and let you know that if you hurt me, he's going to hurt you."

"Well, alright!" I say.

Angela laughs. "Make a left and then the second right at the sign that says Springville Gardens."

I follow her directions. After turning, left, I see the first sign which is Montcrief Park. The second sign at the next entrance is Springville Gardens. I turn in.

"Okay, so you're going to go all the way down as far as you can go. Then, make the left onto Ely Place and you'll see the red house." she says.

"Alright! It's showtime! You ready?" I feel my phone vibrate in my pocket.

"As ready as I'm going to be. And listen... thanks again, Brian. This means a lot to me."

I smile at her as she is smiling back at me. I believe this day will prove to be monumental in going forward with my assignment. As horrible as this situation is, I have to look at it as just an assignment. I can do it and move on to the next one like Dale and so many others have already done. I have to relay to JaQuita how appreciative I am once again for her setting this day up. I'm going to get this done. To Hell with Angela and her kids.

I turn onto Godmother's street and see the red house. The front door is open and I can tell there are already several people inside. I take a deep breath as I park and turn my car off.

"Let the games begin!" Angela says as she gets out of my car.

Indeed.

Angela takes my hand as we walk along the small grass hill that leads to the front door of Godmother Bernice's house. "This is the house I called home from the time I was eleven years old." Angela reiterates that her godmother raised her. She opens the screen door and we enter the house.

"Angela!" A young woman greets Angela as soon as we step in. She comes over smiling.

"Hey Sharene!" They hug and then Angela turns to me. "This is Brian. Bae, this is my cousin Sharene. Her brother is the graduate today."

"Hi Sharene, nice to meet you." I smile and extend a hand toward Sharene.

"Nice to meet you too Brian."

As soon as we shake hands man and woman approach.

"Hello Baby Niece." The man says.

"Hi Uncle Trevor. Hi Aunt Latrice." Angela says. "I want you guys to meet my friend Brian. Brian this is my Uncle Trevor and Aunt Latrice. They are the graduate's parents."

"Congratulations. I know you must be very proud." I say as I shake Uncle Trevor's hand.

"Thank you Brian. Nice to meet you. Welcome." he responds. He hugs Angela as his wife takes my hand.

"So nice of you to come. Thank you so much." Aunt Latrice says.

"I'm happy to be here. Thank you." I say with a smile.

I feel my phone vibrate.

"Where's Godmommy?" Angela asks.

"Where else? In the kitchen of course. She's cooking like a mad woman." Sharene says.

"Cooking? I thought you told me that y'all got a caterer!" Angela says.

"Girl... wait til I tell you what happened with the cate..."

"Oh Lord, look at Angela! Jesus Joseph Holy Mary! Angela got a man! Angela got a man!" The loud voice is from a small woman rushing down the stairs. This must be Aunt Dia.

"Hi Aunt Dia!" Angela says. Everyone around us is laughing.

"You better get ready to be interrogated, son." Uncle Trevor leans over and says in my ear. "This is about to be ridiculous for you."

I laugh as Aunt Dia reaches to hug me before she hugs Angela. "Hello! Welcome! Welcome! Welcome! Welcome! Who might you be handsome man?"

"Um hello Aunt Dia! I'm Angela! Nice to meet you!" Angela says laughing as Aunt Dia gives me a big hug.

"Oh hey Angie. Who is this friend of yours right here?" Aunt Dia says.

"You already hugged all up on him, you might as well just ask him." Angela says.

I laugh. "I'm Brian. Pleasure to meet you. Angela has told me so much about you." I say as she hugs me tight again.

"That's strange because Angie hasn't said a peep about you to any of us, has she?" Aunt Dia says as she looks at Trevor, Latrice and Sharene. No one responds other than laughter. "Angie... you just gonna bring a handsome man around and not give us some kind of heads up or nothing?"

I feel my phone vibrate again.

"Aunt Dia!" Angela grabs her and hugs her to relieve me for a moment. "So this is Aunt Dia. You see why we love her so much."

"Well, I love her too! Pleasure to meet you." I say with a big smile.

"I love him!" Aunt Dia says. "Okay, let me go back upstairs and finish getting ready! I can't be down here foolin' with you all. Nice to meet you, handsome man! Angie we need to talk young lady!"

"Yes Ma'am." Angela says in return.

My phone vibrates.

As Aunt Dia walks back up the stairs, I lean toward Angela and whisper. "Where's the restroom?"

"Oh let me show you." Angela takes my hand. "Excuse us. We need to greet Godmommy. Let's go say hello to my Godmommy first. The restroom is right over there." she says to me as she leads me away.

"Sure! I've been anxious to meet the woman responsible for you." I say as I squeeze Angela's hand. She smiles and looks back at me as she leads me to the kitchen.

Hopefully this introduction won't be as long as Aunt Dia as I need to check my phone. After I greet Godmother, I will hit the restroom and respond to whatever Randy and JaQuita are talking about.

Angela leads me into the kitchen. There are pans of food on the table and shelf. There are pots simmering on the stove. There is a door to a small pantry that resembles what would look like a small closet. Godmommy Bernice is in there as the door is open and we can hear movement inside.

"Godmommy!" Angela says excitedly.

"I thought you must have come in when I heard how loud Dia was with her loud self." Godmommy Bernice laughs and steps from behind the open door. She has empty aluminum pans in her hands which she was retrieving from the pantry. As soon as she stands up straight, our eyes lock on one another and we both freeze. She loses her smile immediately and looks like she wants to lunge at me and rip my heart out. She quickly looks back at Angela and smiles as they embrace in a warm hug. As she hugs Angela, she looks back at me and tightens her face as if she hates me.

"Godmommy, this is Brian. Brian, this is my Godmother." Angela says with a smile.

I stand speechless and motionless. I don't know what to do or say. I open my mouth and nothing comes out.

"Well don't just stand there Brian, we hug in this family! Come on over here and give me some love!" Godmommy Bernice opens her arms for me to hug her. I slowly walk toward her and very carefully hug her. She whispers in my ear as we hug. "It's... nice... to meet you." As we let go of each other, she turns to Angela. "Let me finish this food for this afternoon. The caterer fiasco was a mess so I'm doing everything!"

"You need some help?"

"No no, you and Brian go relax. I got this handled."

"You sure?" Angela asks again.

"Girl, go sit down somewhere!"

Angela laughs as we turn to leave the kitchen. "That's my Godmommy Bernice! My second momma!" Angela smiles. "Oh, the restroom is right there. I'll wait here for you."

Without a word, I quickly walk to the restroom. I enter, close the door and lock it. I immediately take out my phone and see that I have text messages from Randy and JaQuita. They are simply checking in. I send a text not only to them but to include the entire team; Randy, JaQuita, Christine, Dorothy, Carlos and Dale.

THE ASSIGNMENT THREE:
ONE CAN PUT ONE THOUSAND TO FLIGHT

Coming July 19th, 2019

Log onto www.IamAssigned.com to order, starting July 19, 2019.

To watch The Agency Training Video by Dr. Reynolds, please visit www.IamAssigned.com/reynolds

THE ASSIGNMENT THREE

ONE CAN PUT ONE THOUSAND TO FLIGHT

DARRIUS JEROME GOURDINE

THANK YOU

Thank You Father God for the gifts of life and writing. Thank You Jesus for saving my soul. Thank You Holy Spirit for guiding me daily and for helping me navigate the writing of this book. Thank you Kathy Gourdine for always supporting my writing career. I love you. Thank you to Dylan Gourdine for being my inspiration to pursue my God given purpose. This is for you son! Thank you to the greatest graphic designer the world has ever seen, Paul Woodruff for the cover and website design. Thank you to graphic designer Norman Rich for my layout. Thank you to my dear friend Kenya-Marie Farmer for helping me read through and orchestrate this book. Thank you to my editor Amber Carter for your excellent eye! Thank you to my Pastor and Cousin, Apostle Sam Gourdine for praying over me and all the keyboards that I put my hands to. Thank you to the person who took the time to read this. I pray this story has blessed your life and caused you to think. Consider Hebrews 13:2. I pray you will look forward to more works from me.

God bless you all!

Darrius Jerome